THE OMEGA'S MARINE

HOBSON HILLS OMEGAS: BOOK THIRTEEN

C.W. GRAY

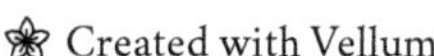 Created with Vellum

ACKNOWLEDGMENTS

Thank you to all the readers who enjoy my books. I love these stories and am overjoyed that there are others who love them too. I would also like to thank my patrons on Patreon. You have helped to motivate and keep me going. Fernando's story has been a long time coming, so thank you for your patience. 😊

CHAPTER 1

"Ican't believe I let you two talk me into this," Fernando grumbled. He rolled his small suitcase through the airport. "I need to save money, not blow it on hotels, food, and beer."

He was nearly done with graduate school; in a month and a half, he'd have his master's in education.

I should be saving for rent while job hunting, not wasting time on a beach, he thought with a sigh.

Months ago, he had thought his first job was secure. The middle school where he was student teaching liked him; the principal had even made an offer. But the school board rescinded it after discovering Fernando's uncle through social media.

He scowled and practically stomped toward the car rental desk.

"You seriously need to get laid," Nolen said, making Fernando grit his teeth.

His dumbass friends had been saying the same thing for months now. *Sex isn't going to magically fix what's wrong in my life*, he thought, but a small part of him argued: *Hell, it wouldn't hurt, right?* It had been a while since he broke up with his last boyfriend, and that ache lingered, leaving him torn between longing and cynicism.

"It's spring break," Gigi yelled and waved her arms overhead. "It's time to party."

Nolen reached over and pushed the sides of Fernando's lips up. "Smile and have some fun, Ferdie."

Gigi turned toward them, continuing to walk backwards. She did her best Cher impression and sang "Fernando" at the top of her lungs.

Fernando groaned. *I never should have started watching musicals with them.*

Nolen shimmied and joined in, ignoring all the people staring at them. He moved ahead of Fernando and danced with Gigi.

"I hate you two so much," Fernando said, shaking his head. "Why do I hang out with you again?"

They finally stopped singing when security started eyeing them. Gigi moved to one side of him, and Nolen to the other.

"You're our friend because we're the only two that haven't deserted you," Gigi said, bumping his shoulder with hers. "You know you really love us."

"Harsh, but true." Fernando had lost a lot of friends over the last few years.

"You'd love us even more if you got laid." Nolen's eyes brightened. "We need to go out tonight. We'll check into our rooms and get all fancy, then go to the nearest bar."

Fernando groaned. "Can't we just go easy tonight? I'm still recovering from mid-terms."

"You'd recover faster if you were drunk," Gigi said, humming that damn song under her breath. "I'm the designated driver, so you get to drink as much as you want tonight, Ferdie. Have some fun and relax. This is our last spring break."

Fernando mumbled a vague response. The semester had drained him; he just wanted it over.

They grabbed a rental car and drove toward their beach-front hotel. Gigi and Nolen chattered in the front seat, excited, while Fernando sulked in the back.

Not sulking—brooding, he insisted to the reflection glaring at him from the window.

He rolled down the window to get rid of that judgy bastard and smiled. He had to admit that North Carolina was beautiful in the spring. The trees were full and green, and flowers seemed to bloom everywhere. It was quite a bit different from New Mexico, though his home state had its own beauty.

Gigi looked over her shoulder at him. "Can't you feel it, Ferdie? Change is in the air, and your new start is coming. The last three years may have been horrible, but I know it's going to get better."

He eyed her suspiciously. "Have you been reading horoscopes again?"

She moved her head from side to side, a serious expression on her face. "It's a good possibility."

He laughed. "At least you're not writing them anymore."

She gave him a serious look. "I would write you a happy ever after if I could, Ferdie."

Damn, I love these two idiots. They really cared about him and had stayed by his side through all the rough times. "I would write you into a murder mystery," Fernando said. "You'd discover the body and be the prime suspect. Don't worry, though. You'd help the police discover the killer and hook up with the lead detective."

"Yes." She punched Nolen's shoulder. "You're probably the dead body. Sorry, Nol."

"My luck," Nolen said, grinning. He rolled his own

window down and stuck his head out. "Damn, I can already smell the ocean."

By the time they reached the hotel, the sun was setting, and Fernando needed some time away from his two friends before he murdered them to rid the world of their perkiness.

The hotel was right on the beach, and he had to admit the sunset over the waves was beautiful. He hurried through checking in and left Gigi and Nolen at the front desk. His room was simple, but it had a balcony overlooking the ocean.

He dumped his suitcase on the bed and went outside, leaning over the rails. He looked to the right and smiled at the dog grinning at him from the balcony next to his own. His room was on the pet-friendly floor of the sixteen-story hotel.

He propped his chin on his fist and contemplated the darkening sky. *What if change never came?* He wondered. The thought of being stuck in the same rut forever terrified him. Still, he hoped Gigi was right, and a change really was on the horizon.

It didn't take long for one of his friends to start banging on his door. "Fernando," Nolen yelled. "They're having a bonfire on the beach and serving drinks. Come on, buddy. No designated driver needed."

Fernando quickly changed clothes. He had hoped to relax before facing another night out, but luck wasn't on his side.

He pulled on a pair of light-blue, plaid linen shorts and a teal long-sleeved shirt. There was a time he would have made more effort, but what was the point anymore? A quick fuck wouldn't solve anything, and no one who knew him would want anything else.

Nolen gave him a stupid grin when he opened the door. "Ready?"

"Let's get this over with," Fernando said, scowling.

CHAPTER 2

$\mathcal{W}$alker Jones strolled behind his buddies as they headed down to the beach. They laughed with an almost manic energy that Walker felt thrumming in his own veins. Tomorrow afternoon, they were all due back on base to check in for their next deployment.

This would be Walker's third deployment. He loved being a marine, but he had started to hate the days leading up to leaving. Some of his buddies were married and spent that time with their families. Some were close to their parents and siblings, and saying goodbye to them was always hard.

Walker had no one. It should have made things easier, but knowing that there was literally no family to notify if he died gutted him.

"Jones, hurry up," Pug yelled over his shoulder. Walker's friend was at the front of the group. He was a good guy, even if he was a manwhore.

The men reached the beach, and Walker took a minute to enjoy the sunset over the waves. The spring night air cooled rapidly, and people gathered at the large bonfire like moths to a flame.

One man in a teal shirt stood alone toward the back of the group, drawing Walker's attention. He moved closer, and the cool breeze carried the whiff of omega. The man was short with black hair and dusky skin.

Dark eyes met his, and Walker froze in place, energy buzzing through him. Those eyes fucking *saw* him.

"Jones," Pug yelled, dragging a giggling man and woman toward him. "Look, twins! One for me and one for you."

The omega rolled his eyes and moved further into the group.

Walker glared at his friend. "Damn it, Pug."

Pug shrugged. "What did I do?"

"You exist," Walker said, scowling at his friend before following the omega.

He was partially aware of Pug turning with a shrug to the man and woman. "Oh, well. How do you two feel about a threesome?"

Walker pushed through the crowd, eyes searching for the omega. He did't understand why it mattered so much or what exactly was drawing him in, but something about the man's eyes felt magnetic—like they offered a connection he didn't realize he was yearning for. A bright stripe of teal caught his eye, guiding him forward.e.

The omega tried to move closer to the fire, but a large alpha blocked his way, eyes looking the omega up and down.

"You need an alpha to fill your hole, omega?" The alpha asked.

Walker winced. *That is the shittiest pickup line I've ever heard.*

The omega glared. "No, thanks."

"Come on," the alpha said, voice low. "You know you want it." He grabbed the omega's shoulder and tried to pull him closer.

Walker growled, rushing forward.

Before he could do anything, the omega snorted, then kneed the alpha in the balls. "Don't just grab people, Alphahole."

The man went down fast, clutching his crotch.

Walker laughed, and the omega looked over his shoulder.

"I guess you don't need any help?" Walker asked.

The man cocked his head. "Aren't you busy with the twins?"

Walker grinned and moved to stand beside him, nudging the alpha curled up on the ground. "That's not my style. Nice moves you have there."

"My brother gave me some lessons." His dark eyes reflected the flames from the bonfire. "I'm Fernando."

"I'm Walker." Walker nodded toward the waves. "Wanna get out of here?"

Fernando made a face. "It's cold, and I'm not walking in the dark with a stranger."

Walker laughed. "Okay, can't blame you for being smart." He waved to a few chairs closer to the hotel. "How about there?"

Fernando nodded. "I can scream really loud. Someone should hear me if you try anything."

Walker shook his head and hid his grin. He should probably feel insulted, but the man was adorable. *Is it strange that I find his suspicious behavior a sign of intelligence?*

They walked together to the lounge chairs and sat. The crowd around the fire was getting larger, and someone started playing music.

"Are you on spring break too?" Fernando asked, brow raised as he looked Walker up and down.

"No." Walker laughed gruffly. "No money for college after high school."

"There's scholarships and financial aid," Fernando said.

Walker smiled. He sounded so concerned. Walker wanted

to rub away the little furrow between the omega's brows. "Didn't know anything about that. Our school counselor was shit."

Fernando nodded, looking so serious. "Mine was really good, but I've heard some horror stories from my friends. What do you do?"

"I'm a marine – a combat engineer." Walker smiled. "It's hard work, but I love it."

"My brother was in the Navy," Fernando said. "He says the same thing about it. How long have you been in?"

"Seven years," Walker said. "I joined up right after high school. What about you? I take it you're here on spring break?"

Fernando sighed and propped his chin on his fist. "Yeah. It's my last semester of school, so I need to find a job. My friends dragged me with them since this is our last spring break."

"Major?"

"Education," Fernando smirked. "Middle school."

Walker winced and leaned back in his chair. "I don't envy you."

"That's what everyone keeps telling me." Fernando laughed.

"We're pretty different, huh?"

Fernando gave him a small smile. "Yeah. I've seen that look in my brother's eyes a time or two. When do you deploy?"

"We check in tomorrow." Walker looked up at the sky. "I'm not worried about it."

"You're worried about something." Fernando smacked Walker's stomach. "Tell me. It's not like we'll ever see each other again."

Walker didn't like that thought. *He's right, though, so why not?* "Here's the thing. I don't have anyone. I grew up in foster care and bounced around to several different families. It wasn't bad, just lonely. The only people I have are a few friends, and they have their own shit to worry about."

Fernando turned on his side and watched Walker. "No one worries about you?"

"Nope. That's a good thing, right?" Walker thought he should say something like that. "Normally, it doesn't bother me. But nights like tonight, right before we deploy..." he trailed off.

Fernando shook his head. "I think it's human nature to need someone to care for us. My parents died a few years ago, and it was devastating. I had my siblings, but it's not the same. Suddenly, I wasn't someone's son anymore. Someone's priority. I can't imagine having no one at all. Maybe some would think of it as freeing, but I can't. Not after having a family and losing some of them."

Walker hated the sadness in the omega's voice. It made something hurt inside him. There was more than sadness there, too. Walker recognized pain when he saw it.

This isn't how I thought the night would go, he thought with a snort. Despite that, he *wanted* to comfort Fernando. He wanted to tell him more about his own loneliness and the fear he felt, but tried to hide. At that singular moment, there was nowhere he'd rather be than sitting across from this man and his dark, all-knowing eyes.

"Do you want to talk about it?" he asked, voice coming out huskier than he intended. "Your parents?"

CHAPTER 3

This was *not* how the night was supposed to go. *What kind of man asks a hook-up that?* Fernando thought, fighting manic laughter. He closed his eyes and felt everything bubbling up. It wanted out. He tried so hard to keep it in, but he couldn't anymore. *Why not spill it all to the fine ass marine?*

"I haven't really talked about it a lot." Fernando swallowed hard and rubbed his face. "Are you sure you want to hear about it? It's really messed up. Their death was all over the news and shit, so my friends know what happened. Hell, after it all came out, I didn't have many friends left anyway."

"You don't have to say anything," Walker said, voice softening. The alpha slowly, almost hesitantly, put his arm around Fernando's shoulder. The sympathy on his face made Fernando want to cry. "If you do, though, remember, we won't see each other again. There's no pressure or judgment here."

"Well, you *did* share with me," Fernando said, taking a deep breath. "Okay, so my uncle, Diego, had my parents murdered because my dad found out he was molesting kids."

Walker's mouth dropped open, face frozen in shock. "What?"

"Dark, right?" Fernando sighed. "You weren't expecting all that, were you? It was a convoluted mess worthy of being on one of my mom's telenovelas. Our family lawyer even told us they plan to make an episode about it for Dateline. Diego was the mayor in our very small town, so it was big news for a long time. Still is, really."

"Shit," Walker said, voice barely above a whisper. "He's in jail now, right?"

"Yeah," Fernando said, shrugging. He waited for Walker's arm to move, but the alpha pulled him closer.

"He killed your parents to hide it?" Walker's thumb rubbed circles on Fernando's arm, and he welcomed the warmth the man's touch gave him.

"When Dad found out, he didn't react right away." Fernando leaned his head on Walker's shoulder. "I don't know why. Maybe it was because it was his brother. Anyway, eventually Dad told Diego to stop, or he'd send pictures to the police."

"Instead, your uncle killed them." Walker's lips brushed against the top of his head. "I'm so sorry."

"Yeah," Fernando said softly. "My youngest sister, Valentina, was just twelve. I'm just happy she wasn't with them when it happened."

"Fuck, that's young."

"It is. Plus, at first, we didn't know it was Diego who killed them," Fernando said, words quivering. "We all thought it was a mugging, so he was someone we leaned on for support."

"That fucking asshole." Walker practically growled. "How could he do that? You lost your parents *and* an uncle in the worst way."

"Right?" Fernando's voice broke. "We loved and trusted

him." So many people blamed them for that. They thought he and his sisters should have somehow known what their uncle was doing and put a stop to it.

"You have your family, though, right? You said you had siblings."

Fernando huffed angrily. His uncle's actions were horrible enough, but Fernando had his own sins. "I do now, but I almost lost them because I was an idiot. In the aftermath, Diego manipulated me into thinking my older brother was a greedy, backstabbing asshole. Instead, *I* was the asshole. I treated Mateo like shit and completely ignored Valentina. Our uncle isolated us from one another, just so he could continue to hide his own actions. Instead of seeing all that, I just worried about myself like a selfish jerk."

"Hey, now," Walker said, voice stern. "You had just lost your parents, too. I've seen people grieving, and it's hard to think straight when your emotions are all over the place. Someone so cold-blooded as your uncle would probably find it easy to use you and the others."

"Doesn't change my actions." Fernando watched the shadows dance across Walker's face. "I told you it was convoluted, right? You don't hear this kind of thing all the time."

"Hey, we've already told each other about the worst times of our lives. Next thing you know, we'll be married," Walker said, smiling for a moment before turning serious again. "Do you regret having a family? Sometimes being alone seems appealing."

"No," Fernando said, shaking his head. His thoughts were strangely settled for the first time in months. "Having family and friends outweighs the pain in losing them," he said, looking right into the alpha's eyes. "I promise."

Walker stroked his face. "That's a brave thing for you to say after all you've been through."

Fernando swallowed hard. "Once Diego's crimes were

discovered, my family and *two* friends were all that stood by me, but without them…"

"You'd be me." Walker linked his fingers with Fernando's.

They were quiet for a moment, and Fernando closed his eyes, enjoying the strength in the arm around him. Restless energy filled him as the music got louder and the crowd larger. He was hyperaware that something was happening. Something important.

Walker cleared his throat. "Do you want to dance?"

"Yes." Fernando jumped up. "Enough serious talk, marine. What the hell do you think you're supposed to do the day before deployment? Listen to a stranger's heavy family drama? I don't think so."

CHAPTER 4

The music was almost drowned out by the noise of the couples dancing and talking around the fire, but the singer's warm voice curled its way down Fernando's spine. He hadn't intended for this to happen.

He had spewed all his worries and troubles on the poor man directly after meeting him. They were things he hadn't told anyone else yet. He had apologized to Mateo for acting like a dick, but no one knew he still felt guilty about it. No one knew he missed the uncle he thought he'd had. Fortunately, things were moving away from therapy time and back to hook-up expectations.

Fuck, he is so damn hot. Fernando ran his hands over Walker's shoulders and squeezed the muscles. Somehow, the alpha's shirt had spread open, revealing a large wing tattoo on his chest.

Walker's arms wrapped around him and pulled him closer. Fernando moved to the beat of the music and slid a leg between Walker's, bringing their hips together. Walker's hands slid from his back to Fernando's ass.

Fernando shouldn't feel so good in a stranger's arms. *He*

doesn't feel like a stranger, though, he thought. Walker felt so strong and real. *These shoulders could hold the world.*

Walker dipped his head, and Fernando felt his warm breath on his neck. He tilted his head, giving the alpha access. He was rewarded with warm, soft kisses behind his ear. A shiver ran up his spine, and his dick hardened.

Walker's hands cupped and squeezed Fernando's ass, lifting him off the ground. Their hard dicks pressed against each other, and Fernando writhed, unable to hold still. He moved, hips pumping, and pulled Walker's face to his own.

He watched the alpha for a moment, mesmerized by the man's warm brown eyes. *I need him.* Slowly, Fernando leaned up and pressed his mouth to Walker's. The man's lips parted immediately, and Fernando slipped his tongue inside, dying to taste him.

Soon, Fernando was lost in Walker's taste and the sensations sending shock waves through his body. *I really fucking need him.*

Fernando pulled back from their kiss. "Want to come back to my room?"

Walker's smile was too damn wicked. "Will someone hear you scream from there?"

"Fuck, I hope so," Fernando said, then frowned, "but it better not be because I'm being murdered."

Walker laughed, and Fernando shivered. *Fucker is too sexy to be real.*

"Come on, big guy. Make me scream." Fernando patted the alpha's chest.

"Challenge accepted," Walker said, and bent to kiss him again, distracting both of them.

"Fernando!" The combined voices of Gigi and Nolen made Fernando wince. His friends circled them, then ran off, singing ABBA's song "Fernando" again.

Walker chuckled. "I take it those are your friends?"

"We love you, Ferdie," Nolen yelled.

"I have no idea who they are." Fernando sniffed and pulled Walker behind him.

Walker fought his grin but lost. "Aww, they can't be that bad."

Fernando scowled. "Let's go before the dumbasses come back."

"Are you sure about this?" Walker kept a hold of his hand, squeezing it. "I won't lie. I want you so damn much, but we don't have to fuck."

Fernando looked over his shoulder and arched a brow. "No shit. If I didn't want you, you wouldn't be coming to my room."

Walker stopped and adjusted himself. "Did you have to say that?"

Fernando snorted and pulled him to the wooden walkway leading to the hotel.

Walker stopped again, this time frowning. "Did you hear that?"

Fernando tilted his head, trying to hear whatever Walker was talking about. A soft whine came from under the wooden walkway.

Walker let go of Fernando's hand and hopped over the rail, jumping to the sand below in one easy move. Fernando rolled his eyes and walked around the walkway, then slid clumsily down the bank to the sand. *Fucking marines.*

Walker was on his knees, ass in the air.

"This wasn't how I thought the night would go, but I'm game." Fernando patted Walker's ass.

The alpha chuckled. "I think there's a dog under here."

Another whine came from under the walkway. Fernando knelt beside Walker and held his phone out, shining a light on the loose brush.

A pair of sad brown eyes watched him. The puppy was all

matted fur and big eyes. *Oh, fuck me. I'm in love*, he thought with a gasp.

"Walker, get him out of there," Fernando said, wanting to whine himself. "He looks hungry and thirsty. We got you, baby. Don't worry."

Walker slid under the walkway and gently pulled the puppy out, wiggling backward. His shirt rode up, and Fernando saw another tattoo.

"You have a tramp stamp, Walker? Really?"

"Caught your eye, didn't it? Doing its job." Walker grinned and cuddled the dirty, fluffy puppy. "Look at those paws. He's going to grow into a big boy one day." Walker cooed at the puppy.

Fernando's heart melted. *Damn him. Why does he have to be so fucking perfect?*

"He's so skinny," Fernando said, feeling the puppy's ribs through his fur. *Poor baby.* "Who would have left him here?"

"No tags," Walker said. "We can take him to a veterinarian and see if he has a chip."

"Most veterinary clinics are closed by now." Fernando stroked the puppy's floppy ears. "Are you hungry, sweetie? We'll take you back to my room and clean you up and get you fed."

Walker sighed, but tightened his arms around the puppy. "Little cockblocker's pretty cute."

Fernando smirked. "Take care of him while I ask the front desk if they have puppy food. Go to room one sixteen."

Walker laughed. "Okay. Come on, buddy. At least we're still getting into his room. You need a name, don't you?"

Fernando smiled, then hurried to gather all the things he would need from the front desk. They were happy to provide him with puppy food, shampoo, and a leash, as long as he paid a pet deposit.

By the time they had fed the puppy, washed him, and

brushed the tangles from his fur, the little guy was ready for a nap. They watched him pass out on a pillow on the floor.

"Well, this didn't go quite how I thought it would," Fernando said, exhausted. He watched Walker stroke a hand up and down the puppy's back. *Softie.*

Walker looked up and smiled. "Me neither. He's cute, though. I'm glad we found him. It gets cold at night."

Fernando pulled off his shirt and leaned back on the bed, spreading his legs. He bit back a laugh when Walker's eyes went straight to his dick. "Night's not over yet."

CHAPTER 5

*W*alker moved to kneel between Fernando's legs, eyes focused on the omega's face. The man's dark eyes warmed as they watched him, and Walker swore they could see into his soul. *He's something special.*

He slid his hands up Fernando's thighs and cupped one hand over his hard, covered dick. He traced the length, enjoying Fernando's panting. "You're sure, right?"

"Fuck, yes." Fernando leaned forward and kissed him, arms wrapping around him. "How can you taste so good?"

Walker grunted, then pushed Fernando back on the bed and slid up beside him. He pulled the packet of lube and the condom out of his back pocket. He was happy he'd come prepared. He leaned down and kissed *his* omega again. *I need you to be mine.*

Fernando helped him out of his shirt, then Walker rolled to his back and pulled Fernando on top of him. The omega straddled him, arching his hips and rubbing against him.

"I didn't expect this, Ferdie," Walker said, hands gripping Fernando's hips.

Fernando snorted and moved against him. "You had a

condom and lube in your pocket, Walker. It's okay. I'm *very* happy with this."

Walker chuckled and leaned up to cup Fernando's face, pulling him down for a kiss. "I meant I didn't expect you. I didn't expect something like this to happen."

Fernando's eyes softened. "Me neither." They awkwardly shimmied out of the rest of their clothes, and Fernando laughed when he fell to the side. "We are so good at this."

Walker hummed and leaned over his omega, hands stroking down his shoulders to his smooth, narrow chest and tight, brown nipples. He leaned down and gently bit one nipple, smiling when Fernando shivered.

Walker took his time exploring Fernando's body, relishing the shudders and moans. He traced warm, wet kisses down Fernando's stomach and wrapped his hand around his omega's hard dick.

Fernando groaned and arched his hips. "Fuck, it's been a long time, Walker."

Walker leaned down and licked the tip of his dick, then started jacking him. "I got you." He cupped Fernando's balls, then slid his fingers to his hole.

He took a minute to open the lube pack, then kissed Fernando while he carefully stretched his omega's ass.

Walker felt so strange. His dick wanted in Fernando's ass, there was no question of that, but something in him wanted to draw things out and make the night last forever. He never wanted to forget the taste of Fernando's kiss or the feel of the other man's hands gripping his ass.

He slowly pushed inside Fernando's ass and started a steady rhythm, ignoring his omega's quiet curses and begging. *This has to last a lifetime.*

"If you don't hurry the fuck up, I'm going to strangle you," Fernando said, pushing Walker until he rolled over.

Walker's laughter turned to groaning when Fernando

started riding him, ass squeezing his dick so damn tightly. His hands went over his head and he gripped the bedframe, holding on and letting his omega take over.

After that, it was just heat and movement. Walker forgot who he was and where he was. All he saw was his beautiful omega's hot, dark eyes and intense expression.

He held on as long as he could, but as soon as Fernando's body tightened and stilled, Walker started coming. Fernando's seed splattered on their stomachs while Walker's filled the condom.

Slowly, their breathing steadied, and Fernando leaned down, kissing him softly. "Damn, marine."

Walker grinned and pulled him down beside him before taking care of the condom.

Fernando pinched his nipple and bit the side of his neck. "Shower, then another round?"

Walker's dick told him to give it a few minutes, then he'd try his best. "I only brought one condom."

Fernando licked the spot he'd just bitten. "I have us covered, marine. You're mine for the night."

THE NEXT MORNING, sunlight fell across his face, and Walker rubbed his eyes, trying to get rid of the burning warmth. The scent of omega made him smile, and he pulled Fernando closer. The man fit perfectly against him. Fernando sprawled out on top of him, still sleeping, head nestled between Walker's neck and shoulder.

A soft woof and a nasty stench chased away his lingering sleep. His eyes opened and blinked, eyes adjusting to the light. The curtains were pulled back, and sunshine filled the room. Walker could see the deep blue waves from where he lay. *I could stay here forever.*

"Woof."

Walker wrinkled his nose and looked over the side of the bed. The puppy danced in place next to a pile of shit. *Well, it's not perfect, but still. Forever.*

Fernando groaned. "What is that smell?"

"Our puppy isn't potty trained." Walker reluctantly let Fernando sit up and pull out of his arms.

The omega held his nose and smiled at Walker. "Our puppy?"

Walker swallowed and avoided Fernando's eyes. He couldn't believe he was about to say this, and Pug would give him shit for sure. "I've never had a pet before." *I've never been in love before.* "This isn't the best time for it. I'm deploying, and you live in New Mexico."

Fernando cupped Walker's face and pulled his head up. "What do you want, marine?"

Walker smiled weakly. "I want the puppy."

"A puppy is a lot of work," Fernando said, eyes soft. He gave a rough laugh and rubbed his face. "This wasn't what I expected to find on spring break."

Walker took a big breath and let it out. "I don't want this to be it, Ferdie. I want you. I want *you* to be the person who gives a damn about me."

Fernando leaned down and kissed him. "I do care about you, Walker. More than I should, considering we just met." He leaned back and took a breath, letting it out slowly. "I think, maybe, having a puppy with you would be worth the work."

Walker whooped and tackled Fernando to the bed, kissing him. He leaned back. "You're my omega?"

Fernando started laughing, almost sounding hysterical. "Fuck, we're really doing this, aren't we?" He cupped Walker's cheek. "Yeah. I'm your omega as long as you're my alpha."

Walker grinned and rolled them around the messy bed. "Get up! We have stuff to get done today."

Fernando groaned. "We have to clean up the poop. What's in that puppy food? Beans?"

Walker kissed him again. "Beans. I like it."

Fernando licked his swollen lips, eyes dazed. "Huh?"

"We're naming him Beans."

CHAPTER 6

Fernando wrapped the tiny green collar around Beans' neck while Walker settled the bill at the veterinary clinic. The puppy licked his chin, long fuzzy tail wagging.

"Okay." Walker smiled at him. "We have dewormer, and he's had all his shots. Ready to go to the pet store?"

Fernando nodded, finally snapping the collar in place. "We'll need a carrier so I can bring him on the plane."

Walker gave him a nervous look. "I hate the thought of you being so far away. I know it's stupid because I'm not going to be here. I'll start the process of transferring bases. It'll take a while, and nothing is guaranteed, but I can at least get it moving before we ship out."

Fernando froze in place and stared at Walker. His alpha looked worried but determined. *He really wants to do this. He really wants me. Me.*

Fernando shook his head and headed to the rental. "Walker, after I graduate in May, I have nothing holding me to New Mexico. One of my sisters will still be living there, but she doesn't expect me to stay close. Hell, I think she half expects me to move to Hobson Hills, Maine, to be near my brother."

Walker opened the car door for him. "What are you saying?"

Fernando sat and buckled his seat belt. "I'm saying that I can move here. I'll have to do extra paperwork to get my teaching license here, but it won't take long."

Walker stared at him. "Seriously? Would you do that for me? Your whole life is in New Mexico."

Fernando laughed, then winced at the bitter sound. "I purposely went to graduate school to put off getting a job because I've been rejected over and over at schools back home. They know what my uncle did. He was a *pedophile*, Walker." Fernando blinked away tears. "One place said they couldn't risk it being genetic."

Walker's face turned red, and his eyes grew hard. "Stupid, fucking idiots. They don't deserve you."

Fernando grabbed his hand and squeezed it. "They don't. Get in the car and let's go get Beans some stuff."

The drive to the pet store was quiet, and Fernando started to worry that Walker was having second thoughts. *What if it is genetic?*

Walker parked and gave him a solemn look. "I'll talk with my superior and get you added to the email list for updates. A few of my buddies are married, and I'll get you their spouses' numbers. It won't be easy, Ferdie. Are you sure I'm worth this?"

Fernando thought of Gigi's words from yesterday. "I'm ready for a change, Walker. If I get to have you, all the better." He leaned over and kissed Walker. "You have no idea how much you're worth, marine."

CHAPTER 7

A month later, Walker smiled at the letter Fernando had sent. It was fun to hear about his life on campus with his two friends. He could still see the sadness beneath the stories of lunches and study sessions, but his omega was working through it.

He chuckled at the picture of Fernando and Beans. Their faces were smooshed together and smiling for a selfie.

"Hey, man. That's your omega?" Pug leaned over his shoulder. "Nice. I like his smile."

"Don't look at him." Walker covered the picture. "Somehow you'll corrupt him."

Sliding down on Walker's bunk, Pug lounged back on his elbows, looking exhausted. Still, he made an effort and wiggled his brows up and down. "Fuck, yeah."

After a day of training, they were all tired. That was their days – training and waiting, then training more and waiting again. Over and over. Muscles sore and nerves slightly strained. However, this was Walker's favorite time of the day. Everyone together, despite being worn out.

"Dessie started a prison store," Pug said. "A bag of chips costs five ciggies and a pod."

"A pod?"

"A Tide pod." Pug shrugged. "All she has are barbecue chips, though."

"Why a prison store?" Walker asked, laughing.

"She's bored." Pug grabbed Walker's picture. "This guy really is cute. How much do you like him?"

Walker snatched the picture back and tucked it under his pillow. "Too much too soon, that's for sure."

Pug snorted. "For a fucker that will do just about anything on a dare, you don't usually risk shit when it comes to relationships. What's different about him?"

"What relationships?" Walker asked, dodging the question. "All anyone wants from me is a quick fuck."

"You never push for more." Pug's eyes narrowed. "This omega is different."

Walker shifted, uncomfortable under his friend's gaze. "Yeah. He's different."

"Then *too much too soon* doesn't matter." Pug grinned. "I like this for you."

Walker flushed. He liked it too. Fernando made him think of building a life outside the military. Of having someone to grow old with. A person of his very own. Being with Fernando in person was a heady experience, and Walker could see the future so clearly, but being away from his omega had given him the space to clear his head. Doubts flooded him, and he began to second-guess every choice he had made. Was he really good enough for a man like Fernando? The omega was so smart, and Walker... well, he was smart in his own way, maybe. Not like Fernando, though.

Pug stuck his finger in Walker's ear, making the man jump. "Hey, get out of your head. I swear, you're worse than my angsty little brother. He's sixteen, so he has an excuse. What's yours?"

Walker made a face. "I'm not angsty. It's just that Ferdie is really smart and going places. Is it right for me to hold him back? You know military spouses have it hard. Meyers has been divorced how many times now?"

Pug sighed, looking put upon. "Fuck, okay, so first, your Ferdie is lucky to have you. You aren't holding him back. He wanted a relationship, too, right? Respect the man's decision. Second, you're not marrying the man. The two of you are just giving it a try. If it doesn't work, it doesn't." He paused and smirked. "But what if it does?"

Walker smiled, thinking about that future he could almost taste. "Fair enough."

"Now, forget that shit." Pug kicked his leg. "For tonight's entertainment you can choose one of two things. Meyers and Steve are running a game of spades or Dessie and her boys are starting a D&D campaign."

"I thought they didn't let you play D&D anymore since all you do is roll charisma to try to fuck everything."

"I promised I wouldn't."

"Dessie believed you?"

Pug smirked. "That's on her. So, what will it be?"

"D&D," he said, after a moment of thought. "I want to see Dessie kick your ass when you fuck up the game."

A FEW NIGHTS LATER, Walker was finally able to video call Fernando. Just seeing the man made every doubt and worry disappear. He wanted a future with the omega. At the moment, though, his omega looked tired. His black hair was tousled, and his eyes had dark circles under them. All Walker wanted to do was pull the man into his arms and hold him until he fell asleep.

"Hard day?" he asked.

Fernando yawned. "Finals are coming up, and I can't afford to make any mistakes."

"I find it hard to believe that you're close to failing any class." Walker shook his head. The omega was organized, persistent, and basically a genius. If he wanted, Walker was sure he could take over the world.

Fernando looked amused. "I think you overestimate my abilities, but no. The problem is that two of my professors are trying to block me from finishing my degree. They don't really have an argument to make, but if I give them a reason to fail me, they'll take it."

Walker's fists clenched, but he tried to keep the anger off his face. That's not what his omega needed from him. "Do you need a lawyer? Pug's cousin knows a guy."

Fernando's eyes softened, and he smiled. "I really, really like you."

Walker swallowed hard, face warm. "I really, really like you too."

His omega's eyes watered. "I didn't know I needed you so much, marine, but it is damn nice to have someone else in my corner."

"I will always have your back," Walker promised.

"I'll graduate, no matter what." Fernando sat up straighter. "I have one professor and two teachers I worked with who will write recommendations for me. In another month, I will be finding a job in North Carolina. Away from this hell."

Walker nodded. "My buddy Steve told his wife about us, and she's already looking for apartments for you. I wish you could live with me, but they don't usually let non-dependents stay on base. I could stay with you, though. If you wanted."

"I would love to have you with me." Fernando propped his chin on a fist. "Fair warning. While my dad would tell me to be a good omega and make you a home, that's never been my thing. How about we work together to make a good home when you get back? Are you up for that?"

Walker grinned. "Fuck, yeah. I've never had a home, but I want one with you."

Fernando looked a lot livelier as he fought to hide his pleasure at the words. "You say that now, but my brother is planning to hijack our video call next week. He wants to meet you. I think his in-laws are already trying to think of ways to get you to Hobson Hills."

"We can plan a trip after you graduate."

"Well then." Fernando looked pleased. "How is it going for you?"

Walker shrugged. "The usual. Pug got us kicked out of D&D, so we're stuck playing spades in our downtime."

"Pug." Fernando shook his head, eyes dancing with laughter.

Walker bit his lip, foot tapping nervously. He had never had someone else to think about, and it was driving him a little crazy. He was up for re-enlistment. Before Fernando, he wouldn't hesitate to do it. But the idea of being with the omega all the time was fucking tempting.

"Tell me more about your day. Did Nolen finally ask Gigi out yet?"

"Of course not. I'm on the verge of interfering." Fernando made a face. "Talk me out of it."

Beans jumped up, settling his paws on Fernando's shoulder. The puppy had gotten much bigger. All Walker wanted at that moment was to be right beside Fernando. He rubbed the top of his head. He had a lot to think about.

"First of all, Nolen is a grown man," he began.

CHAPTER 8

A week later, Fernando hurried up the walk to his childhood home. It was strange to live there without his parents, but both Gabriela and he had needed somewhere rent-free. Gabs was settling into the house with her boyfriend, Eddie, but Fernando knew staying there permanently wasn't for him. Even without considering his marine.

Fernando shut the door behind him and dropped his bags. "Beansie boy, where are you?"

The large puppy skidded around a corner and raced to him with a happy look on his face. Their little man was a mixed breed of unknown origin, with thick, wavy brown and tan hair, big floppy ears, and a short snout. He had grown quickly with food and care and now stood about two feet high.

Gabriela's head peeked out of the kitchen. "I already walked and fed the snot. Don't let him lie to you."

"Are you sure?" Fernando rubbed the dog's sides. "He looks like he's starving."

"Have you seen that belly?" She laughed. "Don't worry about him. Your video call starts in ten minutes."

"Yes, it does." Fernando grinned and ran up the stairs with Beans. They went to his room and hurried to set up his laptop. The first call came a few minutes early.

"Hermanito," Mateo said, greeting him with a smile. "Where's this marine? I have some questions."

"He'll call in five minutes." Fernando narrowed his eyes. "Don't be mean to him. He's not used to families, so he won't know that you're joking."

"Am I joking, though?" Mateo rubbed his chin.

"You approved of Eddie, so you had better approve of Walker."

"Eddie only looks bad on paper." Mateo waved his hand dismissively. "Your marine may seem better, but I'm not promising anything until I meet him."

They bickered back and forth for a few minutes, then Walker's call came in. Fernando's marine looked nervous.

"Hello, sir. I'm Walker Jones."

Mateo arched a brow. "So, I've heard. How did you and Fernando meet? He's been surprisingly close-lipped."

Walker gave them a panicked look.

"Ignore him, Walker. I told him we met while I was on spring break." Fernando rolled his eyes.

"What first attracted you to my brother?"

"His eyes," Walker answered instantly. "I felt like they really saw me. Not just a muscled guy in a uniform."

Mateo winced. "Not all people who are attracted to military personnel are bad, but I've met my share of groupies. Fernando definitely sees you as a person, not a uniform. Alright, so how would you describe your relationship with my little brother?"

"As a relationship?" Walker answered, posing it as a question. "I don't have a lot of relationship experience, but I'm committed to making it work with Fernando."

"I'm committed to making it work too," Fernando said,

smiling softly. "Walker is a good person, Mateo. Can't you just trust me?"

"One more question." Mateo narrowed his eyes. "What does your future with my brother look like?"

Walker swallowed hard. "We haven't talked a lot about it, but I picture us living together. Maybe building a family while Fernando pursues teaching."

Heat curled through Fernando, lingering at the tips of his ears. He could see that too. Maybe a couple of kids eventually. A home of their own.

"You career military?"

Walker looked dazed for a moment. "I don't know. I actually need to decide soon if I'm going to reenlist or not."

"You said one more question, and you already asked it, Mateo." Fernando frowned. "Give my man a breather."

Mateo ignored him. "What are your plans if you don't reenlist?"

"Follow Fernando wherever he goes and support him however I can," Walker answered, eyes wide. In that moment, he looked a lot like Beans when they had first found him. All sad eyes and hope."

"Fuck." Mateo sighed. "I like him, Ferdie." He held a finger up. "However, if you don't reenlist, I insist you move to Hobson Hills. Most of our family is here, and we're close."

"That's where Grammy is, right?" Walker asked.

"Did I tell you about Grammy Wilson?" Fernando asked, trying to remember their conversations.

"No, but she sent me a care package and a letter." Walker grinned. "I really like her cookies. Pug stole the scarf that was in there. He said it was so ugly it was cute."

"Grey," Fernando and Mateo said together. The young omega was married to one of the Wilson grandkids and was known to knit horrible creations. Fernando had his own share of scarves and beanies to prove it.

"Yeah, the letter said Grammy's grandson had made it." Walker blushed. "She sent a lot of stuff and said she couldn't wait to meet me."

Mateo snorted. "All I did was tell them Fernando had fallen for some marine over spring break. That's all Ferdie told me."

"I *may* have told Abel a lot more about Walker." Fernando smiled innocently. "Sorry about that. You'll have Wilsons all up in your business now."

Walker looked strangely happy at the thought. "I'm okay with that. They seem nice."

"Oh, you poor, naïve child." Mateo looked sympathetic. "On your first break, you will need to come to Hobson Hills and meet everyone. That's non-negotiable."

"We were already planning on it." Fernando wanted to pout. Walker was his, not everyone else's.

Mateo smirked. "I look forward to meeting you, Walker." He ended the call, leaving Walker and Fernando staring at one another.

"That went well," Fernando said, shrugging.

"I do want you, Fernando." Walker looked almost desperate. "I want to build a life with you. It's too fast, I know, but I'm certain of it. You are my person. Mine."

Fernando felt that odd bubble of *something* fill him, just as he had when he had met Walker. This was another important moment. "You're my person, too."

Two weeks later

FERNANDO DID his best to ignore the looks of disgust some of his professors wore as he took his diploma and crossed

the stage. The crowd was mostly silent, but his family made up for it. As did Gigi and Nolen. The two idiots whooped and hollered from their own seats. It still hurt. He had respected his professors at one point and had believed he had several really good friends. He knew better now, but he had something to focus on. His future was across the country.

After the talking was finished, he pulled off his graduation hat and threw it in the air with a grin. "We did it."

Gigi hugged him, jumping up and down in her heels. "I can't believe we're finished."

Nolen wrapped his arms around both of them. "No more homework! Thank fuck." He spun them around, ignoring the annoyed students around them.

Fernando hugged them tightly, knowing he'd soon have to find his family in the crowd, but until then, he wanted to hold on to the two best friends a person could ever have. The only thing missing was Walker.

"Did you hear from your marine? I bet he wishes he were here," Gigi said.

"Do you mean, this marine?" Fernando's brother stood behind them, grinning. He held up his tablet.

"Walker!" Fernando pushed his friends away from him and grabbed the tablet. "They let you videocall?"

"Traded some favors to get this time," Walker said, handsome face practically glowing with pride. "Damn, Ferdie. You did really well.Magna cum laude? I bet those assholes in New Mexico are kicking themselves for not hiring you."

"Seriously," Mateo said, scowling. "The middle school in Hobson Hills will take you anytime. I already talked to the principal. Well, Gramps and I talked to the principal."

"Walker can't get stationed in Maine," Fernando poked his brother. "He's necessary for my continued happiness."

Walker grinned. "Hell yeah, I am. Don't make me have to

call Grammy and have her get on to you and Gramps, Mateo."

"Walker has a lot more than just Fernando and Beans waiting on him to come home," Abel said. Mateo's husband held their toddler, Emma, on one hip while their eldest, Iggy, bounced in place beside him. "You don't want to test Grammy right now, babe. She wants to adopt that man."

Walker blushed, making them all laugh. Grammy would adopt Walker in an instant if he'd let her. The woman had taken to the young man from the moment they'd first exchanged letters.

Mateo sighed. "I just want you all close to me. Even Gabs and Eddie, and Gigi and Nolen, here."

Gigi smooshed Mateo's cheeks in her hands. "You're such a big, cute papa bear. Yes, you are."

His sisters pushed through the crowd to reach them. Gabriela looked pissed. "We need to vacate soon, or I'm throwing fists."

"Flipping tables," Valentina agreed, looking just as angry. "I'm glad you're leaving this shit hole, Ferdie."

"Language," Abel said half-heartedly. "You heard that family behind us, didn't you?"

His sisters nodded in unison.

"It wasn't this bad when I graduated." Gabriela took a deep breath. "I don't think I can stay here either, Ferdie. If strangers are willing to be that nasty to my family, I don't want to share a state with them."

"It will die down after a while," he said, wincing.

"Babe, we should totally move away from this place," Eddie said, pushing through the crowd. "I can't believe the things I keep hearing."

Gabriela gave Fernando a look. "See? They don't deserve us."

"A new music teacher and nurse for Hobson Hills." Mateo looked excited.

"Whoa there, big bro." Gabriela held up a hand. "I have a population requirement, so we'll look into Portland."

Mateo shrugged. "Better than nothing."

Fernando turned his attention back to Walker. "Thank you for being here, Walker."

"Anything for you," Walker said, giving him a tender look. "I'm so proud of you."

The day suddenly seemed a lot better. The judgmental idiots around him didn't matter so much when he had a man looking at him like he hung the moon and a family that believed in him.

CHAPTER 9

A month later, Walker came to a stop in front of Fernando's apartment building, turned his bike off, then kicked the side stand down. He was exhausted and anxious. Seeing the omega after months apart was nerve-racking. Through several talks and emails, Walker felt sure of his feelings, but what if being together in person was different? Awkward? Having a person of your own was hard.

He barely had time to get off his bike and remove his helmet before a familiar omega was suddenly there in his arms.

"Welcome home, asshole." Fernando hugged him tightly and glared at him. "Why didn't you tell me you were arriving today? I could have been so much better prepared. Pug only texted me like ten minutes ago."

Walker leaned back and grinned. Fernando wore grey athletic shorts and a bright pink shirt with a UFO and Bigfoot on the front. His usually styled hair was a mess, he needed a shave, and black-framed glasses perched on his nose. Walker loved it. His worry melted away as he hugged his omega again.

"Fuck, it's good to hold you."

"Truth." Fernando buried his nose in Walker's neck. "I'm so glad you're here."

After a few more moments, Walker reluctantly let go of Fernando. "I kind of wanted to surprise you."

"That's all well and good, but today's laundry day, so you're lucky I'm wearing pants at all. I was going to look so good for you."

Walker cupped Fernando's face and gently kissed him. "You look perfect to me."

Fernando's face flushed, and he pulled Walker up the stairs. "Come see our place. Beans was sleeping when Pug texted, but he'll want to see you, too."

"Will he even remember me?"

Fernando arched a brow. "Our son has an excellent memory. Of course, he'll remember you."

Walker laughed and followed him up three flights of stairs and into the apartment. The place looked nice. Better than anywhere Walker had lived before. Granted, he'd been living in barracks for about eight years now, so it wasn't much of an accomplishment.

The small living room, kitchen, and dining room were open with light grey walls and darker grey flooring. The spots of color were in the furniture and decorations. The couch was royal blue, with a fuzzy brown-and-black dog sleeping on it. A green and blue rug lay in front of the couch with an empty dog bed in the corner.

"What do you think?" Fernando asked. "Charlie, Steve's wife, helped me pick out the couch and rug."

"It looks really good." Walker walked around, smiling at the bits and pieces of his omega that were everywhere. Fernando had added his touches in brightly colored abstract paintings and framed pictures of his family and friends. Three of the frames were empty.

"What will you put here?"

Fernando's smile widened. "You."

Walker froze, mind short-circuiting for a moment. "Me?"

Wrapping his arms around Walker, Fernando shook him. "You're my person, Walker. Do you know how important that is? I've never had a person of my own. You have my back, and I have yours. Of course, I want your pictures hanging on my walls. I want every bit of you I can get."

"Me." Walker huffed out a laugh. "You're really mine, aren't you?"

Fernando settled his head on Walker's shoulder. "Yes."

They stood there a while, soaking in one another's presence. The house was peaceful. Beans snored from the couch, and the television played a soccer game. Piles of laundry lined the hallway, and the washer shook as it changed cycles.

Walker wrapped his arms around Fernando and hugged him tightly. *My omega*, he thought again and again.

Beans stirred on the couch, head raising and searching the room. Spying Walker, he woofed happily and rolled until he stood on his feet. Two big jumps, he was right beside them, standing on his back legs to join the hug, tail wagging furiously.

"I love you, Fernando." Walker couldn't keep the words inside any longer. Was it too soon? Yes, but he didn't want another second to go by without his omega knowing how he felt.

Fernando's eyes widened, and he slowly smiled. "Really? Are you sure?"

"Yes," Walker said, eyes full of amazement. "I knew you were special the night we met, but what I feel for you is more than I thought possible. I've never loved someone, Ferdie."

"I love you too," Fernando whispered. "I'm so glad you're home."

Beans barked and jumped up.

Walker caught him and pulled him into their arms. "Damn, he's huge." Walker laughed. "We love you too, Beans."

The large dog woofed, then jumped out of their arms to run in circles around them.

"Want to go on a walk?" Fernando asked Walker.

Even though he'd love nothing more than to sit down and fall asleep on the couch, Walker couldn't say no to both Fernando and Beans.

"Sure."

"You brought your things, right? You're staying the night?" Fernando gave him a worried look.

"Yeah, my bag is on my bike." Walker ran his hand over his short hair, feeling his ears heat up. He knew they were red as tomatoes, but he didn't care. His omega wanted him to stay.

They walked together, hand in hand, letting Beans lead them on his leash. It was still hot, but the day was turning to night, and the temperature would be more comfortable in another hour or so.

"The apartment building has a pool and a hot tub. There's a small balcony off the living room, but our neighbor smokes, so I haven't been going out there much."

Walker liked that he always used 'our' instead of 'my'. "You sure about me moving in? I got approval already, but the barracks aren't terrible if you want to take it slower."

Fernando snorted. "I want you with me, Walker. Fuck the barracks. We have an apartment. What's something you have always wanted to do with your own space? We do have an extra room."

Walker thought about it. One of the reasons he liked his job was because he'd learned so many skills while training. A combat engineer had a lot of responsibilities, ranging from constructing and maintaining roads to employing explosives. His favorite part was, of course, the explosives, but that wasn't something he could bring into the apartment.

He winced. "You said you didn't like cooking, right?"

Fernando shrugged. "I didn't like having to cook for the alphas of the house like my dad expected me to. I'm actually really good at cooking; I just don't have a use for it."

"Do you think you could teach me?"

Fernando grinned, eyes lighting up. "I would love that. Gabs and I cook with Valentina all the time. We're teaching her Mom's recipes. What kind of things do you want to cook?"

Walker shrugged. "Anything really."

"I'll start making plans." Fernando swung their hands back and forth. "Cooking with other people is so much better than cooking alone. Now, how do you feel about doing laundry?"

Walker laughed. "Better than you, I think. That was a lot of clothes in the hampers for just a week."

"More like a month." Fernando sighed. "I hate laundry, but I have to have clean clothes for interviews."

"How many have you done so far?"

"Three." Fernando shrugged. "They've gone well, and I've had one call back. Hopefully it turns into a job."

"They'd be stupid not to hire you."

Fernando squeezed his hand. "I'm glad you're my person."

"Have you thought about my reenlistment?" Walker asked.

The omega looked thoughtful for a moment. "I really think that's for you to decide. How do you feel about staying in the military?"

Walker shrugged. "It's all I know. After I graduated high school, I joined up and haven't looked back. Before you, there was nothing else for me. I think it's the first place I really felt I belonged. Reenlisting feels…" he struggled to find the right word. "Comfortable, I guess."

"How do you feel when you think about leaving it?"

"Scared as shit," he answered quickly. "Excited, but a little panicked. I don't know what I would do. Where would I fit?" He paused for a moment. "I know that I would be here with you, though. That makes everything else pale in comparison."

They stopped and let Beans do his business.

Fernando gave him a worried look. "I can't lie. I want you with me all the time, but I don't want you to come to hate me. I'm with you either way. When do you have to decide?"

"October."

"Okay." Fernando nodded. "Let's see how the next few months go. We can spend time together and go visit Hobson Hills." His worry seemed to fade. "I'm just happy to have you with me right now."

Walker grinned. "You want me to pick up the poop, don't you?"

"Yes, please."

LATER THAT NIGHT, Walker lay with Fernando on their bed. He kissed his omega, enjoying the feel of the man in his arms. When Fernando's lips pressed back desperately, and he wound his arms around Walker's neck, Walker sank into him.

As he kept a steady pace, he kissed his way down Fernando's neck, then nipped his shoulder when his dick hit the right spot inside Fernando.

"Walker," Fernando said, panting. Walker couldn't stop himself from increasing his pace, relishing the feel of his omega's hard dick pressed against his stomach.

He reached between them, wrapped his fingers around

Fernando's erection, and stroked him. His other hand gripped Fernando's thigh, spreading him a little wider.

"More," Fernando said, breathless. "I need more."

Walker moaned and bit down on Fernando's shoulder, careful not to break skin. His grip on omega's thigh tightened, and he felt it coming. Everything inside him pulled tight, but he needed something to push him over the edge.

Fernando spread his legs wide, wrapping his one around Walker's hip. The omega's smaller body pulled tight, and he screamed as he came, splattering against Walker's stomach. He shuddered, body undulating, as fierce satisfaction filled his brown eyes.

Walker couldn't stop himself. He came hard at the sight of Fernando's satisfaction. After his body steadied, he stayed wrapped around his omega, enjoying the feeling of rightness. The room quieted, their pants softening and the light glistening off Fernando's wet skin.

A deep, deep peace filled Walker, insulating him in gentle warmth. That wasn't sex. That was something so much better.

"Ferdie," he said, giving his omega a gentle kiss. "Thank you."

"Yeah, anytime," Fernando said, looking very sleepy. "We need to clean up."

"You stay right there. I got you," Walker said and ran to the bathroom. He wiped himself down and grabbed a clean rag. He couldn't wait to explore Fernando all over again.

Fernando smiled as he watched Walker place the fried eggs on top of the chilaquiles. His alpha was a good cook so far. Even if he needed exact measurements from Fernando instead of his usual *a pinch of this and a dash of that*.

Walker added the remaining toppings, then looked to Fernando for approval. "Is this right?"

"Perfect." Fernando grinned and leaned over to kiss the man. "Cooking is so much more fun when I'm watching you do it."

Walker chuckled. "I like it."

"I can teach you more than traditional Mexican dishes, too, but I've been craving chilaquiles for a while."

"With a cookbook, maybe? For reference?" Walker's eye twitched, making Fernando laugh.

"You really like specific measurements, huh?"

"It seems important."

Fernando wrapped his arms around Walker's waist. "You would get along with Valentina. She hates when Gabs and I tell her to sprinkle a little salt. She wants to know exactly how much and insists it be evenly dispersed."

"Your sister is obviously an intelligent young woman." Walker hugged him back. "When do you want to leave for Hobson Hills?"

"Tomorrow is soon enough. Are you sure you don't want to drive there? You have a whole week off."

"I promised Grammy that I would help her with her garden and Marco that I would help him in the hay fields."

Fernando wanted to tell him that vacation was meant for relaxing, not working, but he looked so excited. His alpha was really looking forward to meeting the Wilsons in person. Fernando hadn't realized how often they emailed and called Walker while he was deployed.

"Anna and Barry both want to teach me some of their signature dishes, too, when I told them you were teaching me to cook."

Fernando's heart melted at the eager look on Walker's face. He needed to remember that having a family was something new to Walker. And it was clear he had family. The Wilsons were eager to meet him. Apparently, Grammy and *all* of her kids were trying to steal his alpha.

They sat at the table, and Fernando scooped up a bite. He savored the texture and taste, enjoying the savoriness and the spice's kick. Walker *liked* cooking. Fernando's dad would have been horrified to see an alpha in the kitchen. Hell, Mateo had to learn to cook *after* leaving home, while Fernando and his sisters were supposed to excel at it *before* leaving home.

Walker looked pleased as Fernando shoveled more food into his mouth. "You like it?"

"It's delicious," Fernando said, after swallowing. "You should cook every day."

Walker's smile lit up the already bright room. A sweet

flutter of happiness filled Fernando. Walker was something special. He knew that from the start. Each second he spent with the man increased the certainty that Fernando wanted forever with Walker.

"I told you my dad had ideas about what omegas should do and how they should live, right?"

Walker nodded. "He thought you should be a *traditional* omega and cook, clean, and grow babies."

"It made me want the exact opposite. He hated that I was going to school, even more so than that Gabriela was going, which I never understood. Most of the time, it felt like he was trying to force us into these roles, whether we wanted them or not. When Mateo didn't fit into the role Dad wanted him in, he basically disowned him."

Walker blinked, surprised. "Mateo is a great guy."

Fernando nodded and took another bite, chewing thoughtfully. "He is. Except he didn't marry Iggy's omega dad when he got pregnant. They agreed to co-parent as friends, but Dad thought that was unacceptable."

"Well, that's stupid." Walker made a face. "I've seen enough to know that families come in all shapes and sizes."

"They do." Fernando sighed. "Seeing how angry Dad was with Mateo made Gabs and me scared to be ourselves. At least when we were younger. I think the only reason he let me go to college was because I was in education. He thought that was a good *omega* job. Being away from him, though... I was just starting to come into my own when he died." He shook his head. "I guess what I'm trying to say is that I may not want to be a traditional omega, but I really want you. I want a life with you. Maybe even a kid someday. I want us to be a family. Even if you deserve more. Someone like Steve's wife, Charlie. She's great, but her life revolves around him and his career. I don't know if I can be someone like that."

Walker stared at him, face flushed, the tips of his ears

bright red. "I don't need a traditional omega. I need you. I want a life where we can be whatever we want, with no judgment. A family. I *want* to cook for you, and I don't mind cleaning."

Fernando smiled sheepishly. "I don't mean you have to clean up after me. I just mean we can do that together. I think I focus so much on it because of Dad. It's really not a big deal. Who actually likes cleaning anyway? No one sane, that's for sure."

Walker winced. "Well…"

"Oh, no." Fernando covered his face. "You like cleaning, don't you?"

"I do." Walker laughed.

Fernando sighed, fighting a smile. "I guess I still love you, even if I don't understand you."

"I think as a kid, it let me control the environment around me a little, which helped since I had to move from family to family so often. As an adult, it makes me happy to have a space of my own, even if it's just in the barracks."

"You have more than the barracks now." Ferdando waved his hands around the apartment. "This is *our* home. You can cook and clean all you want."

Walker grinned. "Plus, Beans can be our baby until you're ready for one, because I do want kids of my own one day. One, two, three. I'll be happy with any as long as I have them with you. If you decide you don't want to go through pregnancy, we could even foster. I think any kid who got to have you as a parent or guardian would be lucky."

That bubble of happiness fluttered through him again. Having his alpha right here in front of him, ready to jump into the deep end alongside him, was fucking enchanting.

"We're really doing this." Fernando shook his head. "I have to keep reminding myself that you're just as into this as

I am. Fuck, now I have to share you with the Wilsons for a week. Damn it."

"We'll survive." Walker watched him eat. "It will be really nice to spend time with your family in person. Barry said you and I would stay at his house. Is that alright?"

Fernando sighed. "The Wilsons really want to kidnap you."

CHAPTER 11

"Why is your friend so strange?" Fernando asked, laughing as he held up a picture on his phone. Pug sat on their couch with Beans in his arms, swaddled like a baby.

"I think he was born that way. I met his parents once. They are just like him." Walker smiled, enjoying the summer breeze as they drove through rural Maine. The scenery was nice, the scents of pine and wildflowers pleasant. Best of all, he had Fernando at his side.

His omega was taking a break from singing along to his playlist of musical numbers to check his messages and let his brother know they were almost to Hobson Hills.

The town was situated between a state park and a few large lakes. Their population was below five thousand, but they had a decent stream of tourists in the summer. Walker had done his research. Why, he wasn't sure, but the way Grammy and the others talked about the town had made him curious.

They drove past a few farms and plant nurseries before the houses grew steadily closer together.

Walker slowed and squinted at the town welcome sign. "Is that Bigfoot?"

The large wooden sign was simple and quaint, with the words "Welcome to Hobson Hills" painted in blue. Next to it, however, was a large, wooden statue of Bigfoot.

Fernando looked up and snorted. "Yeah. I forgot. Mateo said they were having a Bigfoot festival later this week. They must be advertising."

Walker grinned. "That sounds fun."

"They have a lot of festivals here." Fernando smiled softly. "Small towns can be charming when they try. I miss that about my hometown."

They drove slowly through Main Street. It was a Sunday, and a small market had been set up around the town square. Clearly, they were selling something good because the crowd looked rather happy.

"There's Gabs and Eddie." Fernando wiggled in his seat. "Let's park and go say hello."

"As you wish." Walker found an empty spot along the sidewalk and pulled in.

"I'm glad I made you watch *The Princess Bride*. You've learned well." Fernando leaned across the console and kissed his cheek.

"It was a good movie. Much better than Chicago."

"Bite your tongue. No insulting my musicals."

"I hadn't realized you were a theater geek when we met." Walker got out of the car. "I really think that's something you should have told me up front."

Fernando shrugged. "You didn't tell me you liked Dungeons and Dragons until I was fully committed. No one is perfect."

Walker laughed and pulled the omega into a side hug. "Where's your sister at?"

"I saw her at that booth over there."

Fernando led the way through the market, dodging families and pets. The place sold a wide range of items, from delicious-smelling food and homemade crafts to a variety of plants. Walker noted the booth with apple products and the other selling battered fish and chips.

Gabriela squealed when she saw them. The young woman was pretty and looked a bit like Fernando. She was short with long black hair and a curvy figure, and dressed stylishly in a light blue skirt and a white lace sleeveless blouse. The man next to her, Eddie, was her exact opposite - tall, skinny with lanky blond hair, and dressed in shorts and a t-shirt with Bigfoot and aliens on it. They made an unlikely couple. Walker also now knew where Fernando got his laundry day shirt.

She flew into Fernando's arms and hugged her brother tightly. "You're already here! Oh, I've missed you."

Eddie smiled wide and waved at Walker. "Hey, man. Nice to meet you in person. Can I hug you?"

Walker blinked, surprised at the request. "Umm, sure. I guess."

Eddie hugged him close, long arms wrapping around him. Walker stood there, slightly confused and happy at the same time. Fernando was the only one who ever hugged him, and those hugs, while wonderful on their own, were not like this hug. This was warm and safe, comforting even.

Eddie released him a moment later and patted his shoulder. "It's a good thing you got here early, buddy. We're going hunting tonight."

Walker shifted from foot to foot. "Yeah, Mateo invited me, but honestly, I don't feel great about killing animals."

"Oh, we aren't killing anything. That's no bueno." Eddie shook his head. "We're hunting a sasquatch. There's been a lot of UFO activity in the area, and that means it's likely they're here to communicate with their cousins, the sasquatch."

Walker blinked again, processing the man's words. "Okay. We're not hunting deer. We're hunting Bigfoot."

"Yeah, man. Great, isn't it?"

Walker nodded slowly. "Cool, cool. Okay."

Gabriela let Fernando go and turned to him with her arms open. Walker let her hug him, too, again getting that same warm burst of something. *What the hell is happening?*

"It's so good to meet you in person, Walker." She leaned back and looked up at him, smiling happily. "You are definitely Ferdie's better half."

Fernando glared at his sister and pried her out of Walker's arms before taking her place and snuggling against him.

Walker smiled and hugged his omega.

"Fernando, is that you?" An older man asked at the booth with apple products. A short girl with black hair stood next to him, her smile showing off a small gap in her front teeth.

The older man saw Walker and grinned before coming out from behind the booth. "This must be Walker. I'm Gramps, son. You're early."

Walker flushed, excitement and nervousness causing him to practically vibrate in place. "Hi, sir. It's nice to finally meet you."

Gramps wrapped his arms around Walker and pulled him close. "Laurel is gonna kill me since I got to see you first. She's real excited about you coming to town."

Walker pressed his face against the man's shoulder and let himself soak up the warmth. The man smelled of apples and cinnamon, and his arms were strong around Walker. Secure.

The girl from the booth wiggled between them and hugged Walker as well. "Hi, Walker. I'm Olive. My dad and I are the ones who sent you apple chips. I helped make them for you."

Walker laughed, fighting back tears. He wasn't sure why he wanted to cry, but he really liked all the hugs from this town. "I remember those chips. I split them with my friend Pug. We enjoyed them. Thank you so much for making them."

She giggled. "His name is Pug? I like that."

Walker met Fernando's eyes a moment later, and they shared a soft smile.

"Are you hungry?" Gramps let him go, then tugged him to the booth. "Olive, can you get him some cider?"

"Yep." The girl ran to the booth and grabbed a big glass with the orchard's logo on it.

"I'll go get you some fish and chips from the pub's booth." Gramps patted his shoulder, smiling at him again. "Have a seat with Olive, and I'll be right back. Oh, and I see you, Ferdie boy. You'll get food too."

"And a hug?" Fernando asked, chuckling.

Gramps grinned, picked the smaller man up, and swung him around. "We missed you, boy. You and your sister need to visit more." Gramps set Fernando down and hurried over to the pub's booth.

Fernando watched Walker with a smug look. "Maybe I don't mind sharing you with the Wilsons."

The next day, while Mateo was with Grammy Wilson, Fernando lounged on a towel as the afternoon sun warmed his skin. The lake was smooth as glass, and light slid across the water, turning it silver. His youngest sister, Valentina, lay beside him, head pressed to his as she read a book.

Gabriela kicked her shoes off and let her feet dangle over the edge of the pontoon boat. "It's a little too cold for me," she announced, nose wrinkling, as she pulled her feet out of the water.

Eddie sat beside her, shoulder to shoulder. He grinned and slid off the boat, pulling Gabriela with him. She screeched as she hit the water, then started laughing as she immediately tried to dunk the man's head under the water.

Behind them, Mateo unpacked snacks with ceremonial seriousness, lining everything up as if this were a mission rather than a day off. "I have sandwiches, potato chips, and bottled water. Abel sent a few beers too. It's a new recipe, and he wants us to try it. It's infused with raspberries."

Fernando made grabby hands, and Mateo handed him

one. He took a long sip and sighed happily. It was tart with a hint of sweetness. "Delicious."

They drifted through the water, boat dipping in slow, uneven rhythms. Gabriela and Eddie swam beside them, laughing harder each time Gabs managed to dunk Eddie.

Fernando studied Valentina. She appeared to be reading, but he recognized that brooding expression all too well. He sometimes saw it in the mirror.

"You're brooding," he said, trying for a smile.

Valentina looked at him, then sat up, folding her legs beneath her. For a moment, neither of them spoke. The gentle rhythm of the lake and the sound of laughter were all they heard.

"I'm not brooding," she said finally, looking grumpy.

"Yes, you are." Fernando shrugged. "You get this face. Like you're trying to solve a math problem that doesn't have numbers."

Valentina laughed reluctantly. "You're so annoying."

Fernando rolled over onto his stomach, resting his chin in his hands. "So, what's the problem?"

She hesitated for a moment, then sighed. "I don't know how you all do it. You love people like it's easy. Like it doesn't scare you."

Mateo snorted a laugh and sat beside them. "It may seem like that, but love isn't always easy."

Fernando's smile softened. "Personally, it scares me all the time. The more I give to Walker, the more he can hurt me."

"Then why keep doing it?" Valentina asked with a huff.

He thought for a moment. "Because being scared isn't the worst thing. Being closed off is."

She looked away, jaw tightening. "Love makes you stupid. You give someone all the sharp edges they need to hurt you."

"Yeah," he said quietly. "But it also gives them the chance to see every bit of you and accept you."

She sighed. "What if they leave? Or die like Mom and Dad? I know they didn't want to go, but they're still gone, and it hurts."

Fernando closed his eyes for a moment, then shared a look with Mateo. They all missed their parents, but Valentina had missed out on the most.

"I just know that when I love someone, even if it ends badly, I'm still glad I tried. Those moments that I spent with them mattered. They don't disappear just because things change."

"Imagine if you never got to do anything with Mom," Mateo said, grinning. "Remember how she haggled with the butcher each time she bought meat? She went from quiet, well-behaved housewife to raging tiger. That was the absolute best."

"It was so embarrassing," Valentina said, laughing. "I think they both enjoyed it way too much." She smiled. "Remember how she always made us dress up for Christmas day in matching pajamas?"

"Talk about embarrassing," Fernando said, chuckling. "I still have that last pair."

"I miss Dad too," Mateo said, sighing. "He and I had issues, but there were good moments too."

"I remember one time," Valentina said softly, "Dad took me fishing. He said it wasn't something a lady should do, but that it would be our little secret."

Fernando whistled. "He never took me fishing. Was it fun?"

She nodded. "It was quiet, but exciting. I caught a really small fish, and Dad showed me how to unhook it and put it back in the water."

"I miss Uncle," Fernando whispered. "Well, the man we thought he was."

Mateo's eyes watered. "I do too."

"He taught me how to ride a bike," Valentina said softly. "Mom and Dad were busy, but he always made time for me."

"Those memories don't change even if we know his true nature." Fernando sighed. "The pain he's caused everyone is on him, though. We did nothing wrong."

She was silent for a long moment. "Maybe some memories are enough to balance out the pain. Like with Mom and Dad. And maybe it's okay that we loved Uncle. You're right. His actions are on him."

Mateo leaned over and hugged her, rubbing his face against her hair. "What has you thinking so much about love?"

"There's this boy –"

"You're too young," Mateo interrupted. "No."

Fernando laughed and punched Mateo's arm. "Shut up. Tell us about him, Val."

"He's really smart and brave. He's trans, and some of the kids pick on him, but he doesn't let it get to him. I wish I could be brave like that. Oh, and he's really kind. He doesn't let anyone mess with his friends either."

"Have you spoken to him?" Mateo asked, sighing in resignation.

She shook her head. "No, he hangs with the theater crowd, and they intimidate me. They talk so much."

Fernando chuckled. "You should try to talk to him. I speak from experience when I say that the talkative ones need the quiet ones too." He kicked his feet in the air. "Become his friend and get to know him. If something comes from it, then wonderful. If not, then you have another friend."

"What if he thinks I'm stupid?" she winced. "I always say the wrong thing when I'm nervous."

"Then he's clearly not the person you think he is." Mateo

frowned. "You said he was kind. If he really is, would he make someone feel bad about themselves?"

"For no reason," Fernando added, "because you are very much not stupid."

"Maybe." Valentina looked thoughtful as she lay back down with her book.

The rest of the afternoon went quickly. Gabriela and Eddie joined them, and they talked about their dad's old jokes and their parents' half-remembered stories. Eddie played his guitar, a soft Spanish lullaby that Gabriela must have taught him. Fernando's sisters danced slowly as the sun climbed higher, warming their faces. Time flew by too quickly for Fernando's heart.

As the afternoon leaned toward evening, the lake darkened, reflecting gold and pink. They all took one last dip in the water, then wrapped themselves in towels, shared the last of the snacks, and sat close, enjoying the sounds of nature echoing off the lake.

Fernando missed Walker, but it had been really nice to spend time with his siblings. Moments like this didn't happen too often anymore. He wondered what kind of moments Walker and he would have. He closed his eyes and thought about his alpha. The way he laughed without warning, head tipped back. The warmth of his body holding Fernando close at night. The face Walker made when he wasn't sure what to say. His soft quietness that somehow held so much emotion.

His chest tightened, a quiet ache blooming in him. As he had told Valentina, loving someone meant taking a chance, and he would always take that chance with Walker. Love, he had learned, wasn't always a loud thing. Sometimes it was in those sweet moments of quiet, and those moments were worth any amount of pain the future might hold.

The sun set, and the moment of contemplation passed.

Valentina rested her head on his shoulder as they drove the boat back to the marina. "I miss you, Ferdie," she said, rubbing her face against his shirt.

"I miss you too, Val." He looked around. Gabriela and Eddie were curled together, giggling at something on their phones, and Mateo steered the boat, a content look on his face. He wanted more moments like this to hold close to his heart.

CHAPTER 13

Walker stood still on the wooden dock and surveyed the odd sight in front of him. He'd never seen a cranberry bog before. Grammy Wilson's bog was situated between forest, lake, and hayfield and was currently dry. The cranberry vines spread out on either side of the path in glossy, low tangles, their leaves deep green and waxy. Here and there amongst the foliage, the berries were a pale pink.

"They're not red," he said, disappointed.

"Not yet." Grammy tapped one gently with the tip of her finger. "We'll start harvesting in September." She shaded her eyes and looked toward the forest of dark spruce. "When I was a little girl, my dad and I would go out to our bog before breakfast. The mist was so thick you could pretend you were the only people left in the world."

"Sounds peaceful."

"It was." She gestured around them. "Still is, even without Dad."

A grasshopper sprang from the vines and landed on

Walker's boots. He froze. Normally, he'd shake it off, but the quiet of the moment kept him still.

"Don't move," Grammy whispered, delighted. "Oh, I love the little grasshoppers."

"I won't," he promised, smiling down at the small bug. The insect flexed, considering him for a moment, then bounced away into the green. "Does it hurt them? Flooding the bog?"

Grammy shook her head. "No, dear. They like the water, and it's necessary. We flood in the fall so we can harvest. It makes the berries float. In a month, this will look like a proper cranberry bog." She looked down at the ripening fruit. "Right now, they're busy becoming what they're meant to be."

Walker rolled one between his fingers. It was firm and cool. "They're lucky. They know what they're supposed to be."

She laughed, startling a blackbird from the reeds of the nearby lake. "Yes, they do. Sour if picked too early, but worth the wait if given the time they need. Maybe a bit like you."

"Hey," he said, laughing. "I'm in my prime."

She reached over and patted his cheek. "Maybe, but you're still of two minds, aren't you?"

He pretended not to know what she meant, and they walked on. The planks creaked softly beneath their weight. In the distance, a tractor idled near a hay field, low and steady. Gramps waved to them before getting back to work.

"Here we go, then. We need to check for pests." Grammy stepped off the plank path and into the bog without hesitation.

Walker hesitated only a second before following. The softness of the vines underfoot surprised him. "I'm not hurting them, right?" he asked, worried.

"Don't stomp," Grammy said without turning. "They're tougher than they look, but they don't like being bullied."

He adjusted his steps, lifting his boots more carefully. The cranberries nudged against him, tapping his shins.

They stood together, looking out over the stretch of green. He tried to picture it as a field of red, ripe berries, ready to be harvested. "Can I come back when they're red?"

"Of course," Grammy answered with a smile, eyes soft. "You're welcome here anytime, sweet boy. Now, let's get to work."

"Yes, ma'am."

They worked quietly together for a while, looking over the flowering vines. Walker had no idea what he was looking for, but Grammy would occasionally point to a weed, and he'd pull it out before tossing it in the basket he carried.

"Do you do this every day?"

"Twice a week. I have a routine for each day, just like you, young man. Monday and Friday, I care for the bog and gardens; Tuesday through Thursday, I work in the family's store; Saturday, I nose around my children, making sure they're not making a mess of things; and Sunday is family time."

"Don't you get tired? I thought you were retired."

"At my age, work is either your prison or your peace. For me, it's my peace. It keeps me happy and sane."

"I'm afraid of losing that," he whispered. "The military fits me. I know what I'm doing each and every day."

"If you leave, you'll create a new routine." She huffed and pointed out another weed. "It will be hard going from seeing the world as a straight line. Someone points, and you go. It's easier. Eventually, though, you'll have to be the one pointing for yourself."

He sighed. "I like straight lines."

Grammy chuckled. "Real life isn't straight lines. You don't have a single road to travel on. It's more like a garden.

"A garden?"

"Everything's wild and has a mind of its own. Growth is quiet, not loud or dramatic. You can't force your plants to grow faster. You water them, you tend them, and you wait. Sometimes it will surprise you with how quickly it grows, but most of the time it takes ages."

"That sounds complicated."

"It is." She gently smacked his arm, laughing. "Do you like tending to this bog?"

Walker smiled slightly. "Yeah, it's peaceful, and I like spending time with you."

"That's all life is. Tending to what's around you." She smiled at him, eyes full of kindness. "In one of your emails, you said the best part of the military for you was helping folks, remember?"

He nodded and recognized a weed, quickly pulling it out. "A couple of years ago, my unit got to help rebuild a bridge for a village. It was the fastest path for them to reach a water source for their crops, so it was really important."

"You did good." Grammy bent and examined a vine. "That's what I mean about tending to what's around you. You just have to be kind, help where you can, and take care of yourself. If you see a weed, pluck it out. If there's an injured vine, nurse it back to health."

"What if I make mistakes?" He asked.

Grammy's laugh echoed across the bog. "Oh, you will. We all do. Maybe you won't recognize a weed right away, and let it flourish in your garden. Eventually, you'll know its true nature. You just need to learn to do better after the mess-up. That's how everyone learns."

"So, mistakes aren't the end?"

"Nope. They're learning experiences. The end only comes when you stop tending to your garden."

"You make it sound simple."

"Oh, it is simple. It's just not easy." She patted his cheek again. "Very few things are. Now, after we finish here, we're going to visit my granddaughter Janelle's greenhouse. She's going to show you how to tend to the flowers she grows. They sell well this time of year."

"Yes, ma'am."

WALKER CROUCHED behind the kitchen island in a stranger's house, trying not to laugh. Across the room, Janelle stood on a chair, carefully adjusting the last piece of fishing line.

"Is it too much?" she asked, head tilted in consideration. Her curly brown hair was gathered atop her head, and she wore leggings, mud-covered work boots, and a large T-shirt printed with the words *Sometimes I wet my plants*. Her purple cat-eye style glasses gave her a vintage look. Grammy's granddaughter was an odd one, to say the least, and Walker absolutely, one hundred percent loved her.

"I have no idea what we're doing," he finally answered her, shrugging.

"It's not enough," she answered, humming to herself. "Malcolm Reed spent years pranking us Wilsons without our knowledge. Do you know how many times I got blamed for one of his jokes?"

"I do not."

"This is basically community service."

"Sure."

Janelle climbed down and put the chair back where it belonged. "Tomorrow, you can help me switch up the plants in my cousin's flower bed. Right now, there is beebalm next to Noah's hosta plants. I'm going to sneak in a fern. It will look horrible." She cackled. "Of course, I'll fix it next week, but until then, he'll have to live with it."

"I'm not sure that's the prank you think it is."

Janelle gave him a pitying look. "You're new to this, Walker. Don't worry. Big sister will help you learn the way."

"I'm older than you. Plus, Grammy told you to show me how to tend to the flowers the store sells. Not whatever this is."

She ignored him and surveyed their work.

The living room lights were off except for a single lamp in the corner. The coffee table had been moved slightly, so it would feel off to poor Mal. On the couch sat a life-sized figure made of pillows and blankets, dressed in an old hoodie. A baseball cap shaded its "face," and under the brim, Janelle had taped a printed photo of a screaming squirrel.

To top it off, a Bluetooth speaker was hidden behind the curtains, queued to play a low, ominous whispering sound effect, and tied to the front door handle was a thin fishing line that ran all the way to Janelle's hand.

The lock clicked.

They both froze.

"Positions," Janelle whispered, ducking behind the island with Walker.

The door creaked open. A visibly pregnant man stepped inside, juggling a grocery bag and his phone.

"I love you too," the man said into his phone. "I'll see you tonight." He tucked his phone into his pocket and looked around. "Why is it so dark? I thought I left the light on."

He nudged the door closed with his foot. The fishing line went taut in Janelle's hand.

Mal took two steps forward and stopped. "Why is the table over there?"

Janelle shook with silent laughter, making Walker shake his head.

Mal squinted at the couch. "Is someone there?"

Janelle pressed a button on her phone. From the curtains came a low, distorted whisper: "Maaalll."

Mal dropped the grocery bag, and limes rolled across the floor. "Okay," he said slowly. "Very funny."

The whisper came again, slightly louder.

"Maaalll."

Mal's gaze locked onto the figure on the couch. "Cain, honey? Is that you?"

Silence.

He took a cautious step closer.

Janelle waited until he was right in front of the couch. Then she yanked the fishing line. The front door slammed shut behind him.

Mal screamed. Not a dignified shout, but a full-body shriek. At the same time, Janelle hit play on the speaker at full volume. The whisper turned into a cacophony of doom.

Mal spun toward the couch.

The squirrel stared back at him.

There was a long, stunned silence.

"What the fuck?" he said softly, looking around the room.

Walker collapsed onto the floor laughing, and Janelle joined him.

Mal stood there, breathing hard, hand on his chest. "You absolute gremlins."

"You screamed," Janelle said, wheezing.

"I did not scream."

Walker sat up, wiping tears from his eyes. "You hit a pitch only dogs could hear."

Mal looked down at the scattered groceries. Then, very calmly, he walked to the couch and picked up the squirrel photo.

"You know," he said, "I was going to refrain from pranking the Wilsons now that Gramps knew about the other half of his family. And you, Walker." He arched a brow. "Yes, I know who you are. I was going to leave you and Fernando be. You're Wilson adjacent, but I was going to be kind."

Walker and Janelle froze. "You were?" Janelle asked carefully.

Mal nodded. "Now, though. It's on."

"For me?" Walker asked, pointing at himself.

"Not quite." Mal slowly tore the squirrel photo in half. "For *both* of you."

The silence stretched for a moment.

"Mal," Janelle said, chuckling nervously. "Let's not do anything we can't undo."

Mal smiled slowly. "Oh, don't worry," he said, picking up the scattered groceries. "It won't hurt." He paused. "Too much."

Walker and Janelle exchanged a look. "Lock our doors tonight?" he suggested.

"Definitely," Janelle agreed.

From the hallway, Mal called out, "By the way, I'll be telling Grammy about this."

"Shit," they said together. They both ran for the door at the same time.

CHAPTER 14

Fernando lay beside Walker, head on his chest, as he listened to the alpha's steady heartbeat. They were in a guest room at Mateo's in-laws, Barry and Jamie. There had been a loud argument amongst the Wilsons over where Walker would stay, and it had been decided that he would stay one night at each house so everyone would have time with him.

He'll be officially adopted into the Wilson family by Christmas, Fernando thought with a grin. Morning light spilled through the curtains, filtering into a warm, honeyed glow that settled across the quilted bedspread. The bed itself was tall and sturdy, with a carved wooden headboard polished to a gentle shine. The walls were pale sage, with framed watercolor landscapes hanging slightly crooked in a charming, unbothered way. A braided rug softened the hardwood floor.

Jamie had even picked fresh flowers and put them in a small vase on the nightstand. The scent of lavender wafted through the room, tickling Fernando's nose.

Walker yawned as he woke, tightening his arms around Fernando. "I haven't slept this well in years."

"I know what you mean." Fernando pressed his face against Walker's chest. He hadn't realized how heavy the weight on his shoulders had been. Even in North Carolina, he worried constantly that people would find out about his uncle and treat him differently. Everyone in Hobson Hills already knew, but they showed compassion for Mateo and his siblings rather than judgment. Mostly. There were a few who side-eyed them, but they were only a few.

"Our lives would be so different if we lived here," Walker said suddenly, surprising Fernando.

"Different isn't bad," Fernando said gently.

"For you it's not," Walker said, chuckling. "I wish I were as brave as you." He thought for a moment. "I also wish I had your family. You're so close to each other and talk about everything. You argue loud and hug loud. I love it." He exhaled. "I would miss Pug and the guys, but your family would make up for it."

Fernando snorted. "They're your family now, too. Hell, Barry told you to call him Dado, like his kids do. I think you're basically a Wilson now."

A long pause settled between them. Walker looked up at the ceiling. "When Barry asked about kids tonight—"

"He always asks. Even if you're not his kid, he asks. Nosy fucking Wilsons. To be fair, if my parents were alive, they would be asking about kids, too. To them, family is everything."

"Family is everything," Walker repeated, speaking slowly to taste the words. "I just... I don't even know what that means right now."

Fernando leaned up and kissed his chin. "That right there is why it's important. We get to decide what family means now. Not our parents or the Wilsons. Us. We've talked about kids and about fostering. When you're ready, we'll make it happen."

He swallowed. "What if I don't know how?"

"You do," Fernando said. "You show up. You stay. You do your best."

He let out a quiet laugh. "That's it? That's the big secret?"

"That's the big secret."

"Grammy said something similar. Something about a garden and life. I don't know." He ran his hand along Fernando's back. "I'm scared I'll mess it up."

"You will," Fernando said. "I will too. But we'll mess it up together."

The tension in Walker's shoulders eased, just a little, and Fernando kissed his chin again. "Now, get up. The Bigfoot festival starts today, and Mateo will want you to go on a hunt with him again tonight."

"Big day." Walker grinned. "Come with me?"

"To the festival? Yes. To the hunt? Absolutely not."

~

A FEW HOURS LATER, they stood together in the crowd, the August heat warming them. A banner stretched over Main Street, its corners fluttering lazily in the breeze. "Welcome to the 1st Annual Bigfoot Festival" was written in large bold letters.

Fernando fanned himself with a folded brochure. "I can't believe so many people came to Hobson Hills for this."

Walker grinned, tugging the sides of his brand-new knitted Sasquatch hat lower over his brow. The thick yarn was too warm for summer, but he didn't want to take it off. Ernie Wilson had given it to him. "You say that now, but they're about to start the Authentic Bigfoot Call Competition. That's culture."

"Culture?" Fernando laughed. "This is a town full of grown men howling into the woods."

A whistle blew near the makeshift stage in the town square. Kids with painted-on sasquatch faces chased each other between booths selling wooden carvings, knitted goods, and various Bigfoot paraphernalia. Janelle even had a booth selling plants in ceramic sasquatch flowerpots.

Walker reached for Fernando's hand as they wove through the crowd. "Okay, but admit it. This is kind of amazing."

He softened, squeezing Walker's fingers. "It's aggressively charming."

They stopped at a booth where an older woman with a squatch watch visor displayed plaster casts of enormous footprints.

Fernando leaned closer. "These look suspiciously like someone stepped in cement with a snowshoe."

The woman overheard. "Sweetheart, Bigfoot doesn't need snowshoes. He's got natural flotation."

Walker nodded solemnly. "Science."

Fernando bit back a smile until they'd stepped away. "You are enjoying this way too much."

"Because it's ridiculous," Walker said, laughing. "And nobody here cares that it is. Look at them." He gestured to a group of teenagers arguing earnestly over blurry photos pinned to a corkboard. "They want to believe. That's kind of sweet."

A man climbed onto the stage and tapped the mic. "Contestants for the Bigfoot Call, please line up!"

Walker's eyes lit up.

"Oh no," Fernando said immediately, tightening his grip on Walker's hand. "Absolutely not."

"It's tradition," Walker insisted.

"You've been here exactly twelve minutes, and this is literally the first Bigfoot festival the town has had."

Walker leaned close, his voice dropping. "If Bigfoot is out there, Ferdie, he deserves to hear my voice."

He stared at Walker for a long moment, then laughed, full and bright and unguarded. "Fine. But if you embarrass me, I'm telling everyone you cried during that documentary about orcas in captivity."

"That shit was moving." He jogged toward the stage before Fernando could change his mind.

Fernando stayed back in the shade of an oak tree, watching as he lined up beside a burly man in camouflage and a seven-year-old girl with glittery face paint. Unsurprisingly, Mateo, Eddie, and Ernie Wilson were also on stage.

"Why is my family so weird?" he asked.

"Because they're connected to you," Gabriela answered him, startling him.

He squeaked in surprise and spun around. Gabs, Valentina, Abel, and the kids joined him under the tree. Iggy's pet bearded dragon, Pudding, was on a leash.

"I thought you had a booth to work?" he asked Abel.

"Gramps is watching it for me. I didn't want to miss this spectacle." Abel grinned. "Mateo's sasquatch call is sexy, you know."

Even baby Emma made a face at that.

"You're disgusting," Val said and pulled Fernando down to sit next to her in the grass. She brought Pudding onto her lap. "You let Walker go up there? What's wrong with you?"

"I was blinded by his shoulders."

Valentina shrugged. "That's fair."

When it was Walker's turn, he stepped up to the mic, cleared his throat dramatically, and let out a long, wavering howl that started low and climbed into something surprisingly melodic. It echoed off the brick storefronts and rolled toward the trees beyond town.

The crowd went silent for half a second.

Then someone whooped. A dog barked. Laughter rippled through the park.

Fernando felt his chest tighten in that familiar way it did when he remembered exactly why he loved Walker. He was ridiculous, yes, but fearless about it.

Walker jogged back toward him, flushed and triumphant. "Well?"

"You sounded like a lovesick coyote."

"Perfect. That's exactly what Bigfoot goes for."

"Walker, that was great," Ernie said. He, Eddie, and Mateo joined them after their own calls. "You are definitely doing the calls tonight.

"Okay." Walker agreed easily. "Ferdie, can we go to the hair analysis lecture next?"

"Please tell me you aren't getting caught up in Bigfoot."

Walker gave him a sheepish look. "It's just nice to think there might be something wild and unknown left out there in the world."

Fernando sighed and cupped his alpha's face in his hands. "They've corrupted you, but I still love you. Okay, let's go to the lecture thing."

"Babe?" Eddie gave Gabriela a hopeful look. "Juan is the one giving the lecture, and he's totally my bro. I need to support him."

She groaned. "Fine. We'll go too."

Valentina scoffed. "You two are way too soft."

A boy about her age walked past them with friends. He had short brown hair and lovely blue eyes. The group was heading directly to the tent where the lectures happened.

"Well, now that I think about it, maybe it's a little inter-esting," Valentina said, eyes following the boy.

Fernando and Mateo exchanged a look. They spoke with

their brows and eyes. Yes, they would both be on guard during the stupid lecture. Fernando recognized theater people when he saw them. They were his people; he knew them well. That boy was the one Valentina liked.

CHAPTER 15

The next day, Fernando was spending time with Valentina, and Walker was back at Mal's house with Janelle. They were there to pay their dues by appearing on Mal's cooking show. Now that he knew about it, Walker was kind of excited to watch all the past episodes. Cooking was turning out to be more fun than he had expected.

"Where did that come from?" Janelle asked in a whisper, side-eying the taxidermied squirrel in the foyer wearing a knitted dress and a pearl necklace.

"It was not there the last time we were here," Walker answered, also whispering.

"It's for Walker," Mal said, startling them with his sudden appearance. The man was dressed to cook, wearing a tie-dye headwrap and a purple T-shirt that said *Will Cook for Kisses*. "Grandpa Paul and Grandma Kat wanted him to have something nice to welcome him to the family. Their words, not mine."

"The Reed side of the family can't have him." Janelle grabbed his arm. "He's ours."

The squirrel's glass eyes followed Walker in a way that felt judgmental.

"Too late." Mal shrugged. "He has a squirrel now."

"At least they didn't send me another one," Janelle said, sounding relieved. "That farmer squirrel they sent me is great. I have it displayed in my greenhouse. This one, though, is just weird."

Walker turned to look at her, blinking slowly. "This one is weirder than a taxidermied squirrel dressed like a farmer?"

She scoffed and gave him a pitying look. "Of course it is, Captain Obvious."

Now that Mal and Janelle were standing side by side, Walker could easily spot the family resemblance, especially in their personalities.

From the kitchen came a loud clang and a woman's voice shouting. "Mal, tell them to hurry up. I'm fermenting something experimental."

Walker paused. "Experimental?"

Mal winced. "That's Bia. It's probably fine. Last time, only two jars exploded."

Before Walker could process that, a teenager with curly brown hair burst into the hallway, wiping her hands on a dish towel covered in mushrooms. "You must be Walker," she said with a smile, pulling him into a hug that smelled of vinegar and rosemary. "I've heard everything about you. Good job with the prank, by the way. Mal totally deserved it."

Walker blinked. "He told you about that?"

"Yep. He was proud of you two."

"Bianca," Mal said, drawing her name out as he stomped his foot. "I told you not to tell them that."

She shrugged with a smirk and went back to the kitchen. "I'll move my jars, and we can start the show."

"Bring the squirrel, Walker." Mal smiled sweetly. "It will be your personal assistant."

"Really?" he asked with a sigh.

Janelle nudged him with her elbow. "This is better than the alternative. We don't want to be looking over our shoulder forever, waiting for Mal to prank us back."

"Smart woman," Mal smirked.

A few moments later, they all stood in a large kitchen with several cameras watching them. Mal had them hanging from each corner of the room, the fridge, and the center light fixture. The red lights blinked on.

"Are we live?" Walker whispered out of the corner of his mouth, smiling so hard his cheeks ached. He held his taxidermied squirrel in one arm.

"The cameras have been recording for one full minute," Bianca said. "So, if you're going to panic, do it charmingly."

"Don't worry about a thing, Walker. We aren't live, and I edit thoroughly." Mal faced forward, palms flat on the butcher-block counter. Copper pans hung behind them, and a pot of water boiled on the stove. The kitchen glowed warm and gold.

"Welcome back to *Simply Living*," Mal said, voice smooth as whiskey. "I'm Malcolm Benson, and today's episode is special because instead of pretending I cook like this every day for imaginary friends, I've invited some real ones."

Walker, Janelle, and Bianca moved to stand next to him at the island.

"We don't know what we're making," Janelle told the camera, already sipping from a glass of white wine she'd found somewhere.

"That's not true," Mal said with a smile. "We're making rosemary lemon chicken with roasted potatoes and a summer tomato salad."

Janelle leaned on the island. "For the record, all he told us was to come over hungry and camera-ready. That's it."

"My name is Walker," Walker said suddenly, blinking nervously.

Bianca snorted a laugh and patted his back. "Yes, it is, big guy. I'm Bianca, Mal's daughter from another life, and that there is Janelle."

"You're too sweet." Mal patted Walker's cheek. "Now that the intros are out of the way, let's proceed." He clapped his hands once. "Okay. First step: Preheat your oven to 400 degrees. Walker, that means you turn the dial behind you."

Walker stared at the stove like it had personally offended him. "Wait. Why is it analog? That's too outdated for a professional. Even Ferdie and I have a new digital model."

"You sound like my husband. It builds character, okay," Mal said, rolling his eyes.

"It builds lawsuits," Janelle muttered, but she was already zesting a lemon into a bowl, bright curls of yellow falling like confetti.

"I like it better than a digital model because it's more reliable," Mal said with a pout. He crushed garlic with the flat of his knife, and the sharp, clean scent rose into the air, followed by the scent of chopped rosemary. "Ignore them, my lovely audience. Cooking with friends," Mal said to the camera, "is about controlled chaos. You want enough people to make it lively, but not so many that someone sets a towel on fire."

Walker froze, holding a dish towel dangerously close to a burner. "Yeah, let's not do that."

"As usual, I sourced as much of my ingredients locally as I could. Hobson Hills has a lovely little store called *Farm Fresh,* which is where I get most of my produce." Mal passed the bowl of marinade to Bianca. "Olive oil, lemon zest, juice, garlic, rosemary, salt, pepper. Give it a stir."

Bianca did, efficient and focused. "You're actually measuring today. That's new."

"I usually measure on camera," Mal said, sniffing, nose in the air. "Off camera, I follow my heart."

"That's how you end up with cinnamon chili," Walker said, wincing at the memory. "Recipes are exact for a reason."

"Cinnamon chili? Now, that sounds experimental," Mal said, grinning.

"It was inedible." Walker sighed. "I warned Ferdie, but he flew too close to the sun."

Janelle laughed, grinning like a loon. "I kind of want to try it."

"I do too. That might make it into my experiments this week. If dinner isn't good, I can blame it on Fernando."

Walker winced again, feeling like he had tossed his omega under the bus.

"Now, this chicken comes from a local ranch and is free-range. There are no preservatives or chemicals in this lovely meat. Simple ingredients mean healthier living," Mal said.

Walker tilted his head, intrigued as he watched Mal cook.

"Walker, pat these chicken thighs, please."

Walker did as he was told, Mal, looking over his shoulder. "Pro tip," Mal said. "Dry skin equals crispy skin. Moisture is the enemy of crunch." Mal guided Walker through the rest of the process. "Slide the chicken into the bowl of marinade and coat each piece thoroughly."

The scent grew deeper and more delicious. Walker breathed it in and smiled. Maybe it wasn't working with explosives, but cooking was still interesting. And less deadly.

"Let it sit at least twenty minutes," Mal said. "Which is perfect, because that's exactly how long it takes for Bianca to start arguing about something."

"I don't argue," Bianca protested.

"Sorry. I meant that you debate aggressively," Mal corrected.

Janelle crossed her arms. "What are we debating aggressively about today?"

Mal smiled. "Best summer food."

"Tomatoes," Bianca said instantly.

"Grilled corn," Janelle countered.

"Hot dogs," Walker said. "Classic. No notes." He had very few good memories of his childhood, but one of them involved one of the nicer foster families he had been with and a trip to the state fair. Hot dogs featured prominently in that memory.

"Oh, I don't know. Hot dogs are a good summer food, but watermelon is cold, sweet, and perfect in the summer." Mal placed the marinated chicken, skin-side up, in a cast-iron skillet, carefully arranging it.

"That's dessert," Bianca protested.

"It's emotional support fruit." Mal stuck his tongue out at her.

While they waited for the chicken, Mal showed Walker how to put together the roasted potatoes. It was easy. The potatoes went into a bowl along with olive oil, salt, and cracked pepper.

Walker tossed them with his hands, trying to be gentle. "Am I doing this right?" he asked.

"There's no wrong way," Mal said, patting his shoulder and giving him a soft look.

Bianca raised an eyebrow. "That is absolutely not true. You tell me I do it wrong all the time."

Mal shrugged. "Okay, there are wrong ways, but Walker isn't doing any of them."

Walker ignored Bianca's indignant squawk and spread the potatoes around the chicken.

"Perfect, Walker." Mal slid the skillet into the oven with a practiced motion. "Now," he said, dusting off his hands, "we make the salad."

Tomatoes in shades of red and gold hit the cutting board. Walker sliced them cleanly, juice pooling bright and glossy. *Aww, knives,* he thought happily. He had thoroughly enjoyed his close combat training, especially knife-fighting.

Bianca tore basil with exaggerated delicacy while glaring at him.

"Why can't I cut it?" he asked.

"Because you'd dice it into oblivion." She eyed the tomatoes. "You look a little too happy with that knife."

"Ignore her, Walker. You are doing just fine. Janelle, put the wine down and drizzle olive oil over the tomatoes."

Janelle kept her wine glass in hand and grabbed the olive oil. "It's so simple," she said. "You cut it, mix it, drizzle it."

Mal nodded. "Simple is the point, but how many glasses of wine have you had?"

Janelle thought for a moment. "Mauve, I think."

"That's not a number," Walker said, fighting a smile. For a moment, the cameras faded into the background, and it was just the four of them around a counter, hands moving, shoulders brushing. The low hum of the oven filled the pauses between words. Walker loved it.

He cleared his throat. "Hey. I know we joke, but this is cool. What you're doing, Mal. I'm seriously going to watch your backlog. I think Ferdie will like food like this."

"Don't forget to invite us to dinner too, Walker," Janelle said.

Mal nodded solemnly. "I couldn't do this show without taste testers. You need some too, and here we are."

"You'll be my guinea pigs?" Walker asked, surprised.

"Premium guinea pigs," Bianca said. "Top-notch quality, right here."

The timer chimed. Mal opened the oven, and the kitchen filled with the smell of roasted lemon and crisping skin. The chicken was golden, edges caramelized. The potatoes had turned bronze.

Janelle gasped. "Okay. That smells illegal."

"Rest it for five minutes," Mal instructed, setting the skillet on the stove. "Patience adds flavor."

Walker peered at the camera. "Write that down."

They plated everything together. Chicken first, then potatoes, then a side of tomato salad with basil.

Mal turned back to the camera one last time. "This," he said, "is what food's about. It's not perfection. It's not fancy plating or knowing every technique. It's inviting people into your kitchen, even if your kitchen has studio lights and a slightly judgmental taxidermied squirrel."

"Extremely judgmental," Bianca corrected as they all looked at the squirrel on the counter.

Mal smiled. "Make something simple. Share it. Burn a towel if you have to."

Janelle raised her wine glass. "To not burning towels."

"To crispy skin," Walker added, practically drooling as he sniffed his plate. He raised his fork.

"To measuring on camera only," Bianca said, raising her own fork.

Mal lifted his fork. "To friends."

They clinked glass and forks together awkwardly, laughing as they dug in. The chicken melted under the knife. Janelle moaned dramatically at the first bite. It was a great meal.

ON THEIR LAST night in Hobson Hills, after dinner with Fernando's family and a few additional Wilsons, they were ushered outside for what Eddie described as casual stargazing, which turned out to involve matching silver cloaks, tinfoil hats, and a telescope pointed toward the stars.

Abel brought folding chairs. Mateo brought a tuning fork in case the sky needed encouragement. What that meant was anyone's guess. Gabriela passed around mugs of something warm and cinnamon-heavy. The family's dogs and cat ran around them for a few minutes before stretching out beside them.

Walker sat between Fernando and the taxidermied squirrel, which had been relocated outdoors for fresh air. He watched Fernando's family argue gently about constellations. Iggy insisted one cluster was clearly shaped like a goat in a business suit, but Valentina insisted it was a dragon. Mateo started a speech about how Bigfoot and aliens were connected, solemn face one of a true believer.

Walker felt something unexpected settle in his chest. This family, well, the whole town really, was loud, strange, and completely unbothered by being strange. He wanted to stay there forever.

Fernando nudged him. "You don't have to pretend to enjoy this. We can grab Emma, go inside, and play with Pudding."

"I'm not pretending," he said.

Fernando looked happily surprised. "Are you sure?"

"The military, which is kind of like my family," Walker began carefully, "likes things tidy. Predictable. We don't howl like Bigfoot, do cooking shows, or dress taxidermied squirrels."

"That sets a low bar," Fernando said, wincing.

"We also don't laugh like this." He gestured to Eddie, who had begun to make tinfoil hats. Walker couldn't help but chuckle. "This is great. Your whole family, Wilsons included, because they for sure include you, are great."

Fernando was quiet for a moment. "I always worried I'd scare someone off."

Walker turned to him. "This? These people right here? They are perfect, Ferdie."

"My uncle sure isn't," Fernando said softly so only Walker could hear.

"He isn't part of this. You said we got to make our own family, right? Well, this is it. Right here."

Fernando leaned his head on Walker's shoulder. "Our family is this right here, huh? Not my parents or uncle, not the military. Just these weird people right here."

Walker nodded. "And I love them. I love this."

Fernando blinked. "You do?"

"I do." Walker grinned. "The only thing missing is Beans and maybe Pug."

"Definitely Beans and *possibly* Pug." Fernando laughed softly. "I love you, Walker."

"I love you too." He kissed the top of Fernando's head.

Under a sky full of misidentified constellations and gentle chaos, he realized something simple. He wasn't scared anymore, or worried, or doubtful. If not, when he left the military, he would flounder a bit as he searched for work and a new routine for his life. That was okay, though, because he had Fernando beside him and a whole lot of wonderful people around them.

Since he was going to build a life with Fernando, he suspected it would include Bigfoot hunts, cranberry harvesting, and maybe a cooking club. It would be here, in Hobson Hills, so they could keep an eye on Valentina's crush and he could help Janelle pseudo-prank her family.

Fernando grabbed his hand and squeezed it. They leaned into one another and watched stars while the squirrel beside him judged them all.

CHAPTER 16

Two months later, Fernando stood in the bathroom and fought a panic attack. The bathroom light was too bright for six in the morning. He squinted at his reflection, hair tangled from sleep. The house was quiet, and Beans was still sleeping. Walker's unit was deployed for training again, luckily, a much shorter one this time. He was set to return in another week.

The pregnancy test lay on the counter.

He had promised himself he wouldn't look right away. Instead, he washed his hands. Breathed. Counted to thirty.

"That's long enough." He looked. Two pink lines.

For a moment, nothing happened. He was still Fernando. It was just that the world had tilted and forgotten to keep spinning. That's all.

"No," he whispered automatically, hoping the words could change something. He picked it up and turned it toward the light, hoping it would reveal a different answer. Nope. The lines were still there.

His chest tightened, and his stomach dropped, then fluttered. A baby. He sat down on the edge of the tub, knees suddenly giving out. His thoughts began racing ahead to the doctor appointments, tiny clothes, his siblings' faces, *his* face. Oh God. His face.

Tears welled up without warning, and he pressed his hand to his mouth and let out a shaky breath. "I'm pregnant," he said to the empty bathroom, giving the words a try.

The words made it suddenly very real. They hadn't planned this. They were still figuring things out. Walker had another six months left in the military and had no idea what he would do afterward. Fernando had only just started the new school year. They were planning to move to Hobson Hills next summer. Fuck, he still sometimes felt like he was pretending to be an adult.

However, beneath the fear was something else. A warmth. A flicker of awe. His hand drifted to his stomach, still flat, still ordinary. Nothing had changed, but everything had changed. There was something there. The tiniest, faintest beginning of a life.

A laugh bubbled up through his tears. "Oh, fuck me," he murmured, laughing and crying at the same time. He looked at the test again, then at himself in the mirror. "I'm okay," he managed, voice wobbling. He stood, wiped his cheeks, and opened the door. Everything would be alright.

He went through his morning routine in a daze, walking Beans, feeding Beans, petting Beans, feeding himself, searching for his keys. Then he drove to work. The school he taught at was across town, and traffic sucked.

Somehow, he made it to his classroom and through homeroom. His first class, though, was a little challenging.

He blinked at the whiteboard like it had personally betrayed him. "Okay," he said slowly, marker hovering over the board. "So. Symbolism. In chapter... in chapter..." He glanced down at the book in his hand.

Several students helpfully chimed in at once.

"Seven."

"Eight."

"Fourteen, if you actually did the reading," griped Alisha from the back.

Fernando squinted at the cover. *The Outsiders*. Right. He absolutely knew that. "Chapter seven," he repeated with forced confidence, turning back to the board. He wrote a large, slightly slanted 7. Then he stared at it, hoping it would continue the lesson for him.

A baby. I'm having a baby.

The classroom hummed with middle school energy, desks squeaking, someone tapping a pencil like a woodpecker, and a crumpled paper ball arcing lazily toward the trash can and missing by a mile.

"Mr. Medina?" asked Alisha, hand raised but already talking. "Are we still doing the essay today?"

The word essay seemed to travel across the room in slow motion before colliding with his brain. "Essay," he asked faintly. "Yes. No. I mean, eventually." He rubbed his forehead, leaving behind a faint smear of dry-erase marker. "First, we're discussing the fire scene."

A hand shot up again. "Why did you write Chapter Seven if the fire is in Chapter Six?" asked Alisha.

Fernando slowly turned back to the board. The large 7 stared back at him, smug.

"Excellent question," he said, nodding gravely. "That was a critical thinking exercise."

His class did not believe him.

He erased the 7, then paused mid-swipe, staring at the half-erased number like it was a philosophical dilemma. *I'm going to have a baby. Another living being that I'm responsible for.*

For a full five seconds, no one spoke.

"Sir," said Alisha, "are you okay?"

He blinked again, doing his best to gather his thoughts.

"I'm fantastic," he said too brightly. "Thriving. Life is good."

A few students laughed.

"Okay," he said finally, closing the book with a soft thud. "Group discussion."

A ripple of excitement passed through the room.

"Talk to your partner about what the fire symbolizes. Five minutes. Use textual evidence." He pointed vaguely around the room. "And stay seated."

The class erupted into conversation instantly.

Fernando leaned against his desk, breathing slowly. He watched as Alisha animatedly explained something with wild hand gestures while another student flipped pages frantically. A paper ball narrowly missed his shoulder.

Despite the fog in his brain, a small smile tugged at his mouth. They were engaged. Loud, chaotic, occasionally feral, but engaged.

Alisha waved at him from her desk. "You should drink coffee, Mr. Medina," she advised.

He nodded solemnly. "You're wise beyond your years."

The bell rang, slicing through the noise. Chairs scraped back, and students poured out into the hallway in a rush of chatter and sneakers.

Fernando remained where he was, staring at the half-erased smear on the board. He sighed and picked up the marker again. "Okay," he muttered to himself. "Chapter six. Fire. Symbolism. You absolutely know this." He wrote "Fire = ?" on the board.

After another class ended, he finally got a lunch break. Before he could leave to meet the friends he ate lunch with, the principal's assistant, Lester Sherry, came to his door. "Mr. Medina, the principal needs to speak to you."

Fernando swallowed hard. *This can't be good.* Principal Nester was strict and no-nonsense. She kept a tidy school and expected much from her teachers. He knew he hadn't been at his best that morning, but she wouldn't know that. Right?

He suddenly felt like he was twelve again. "Uh, sure. I'll head to her office."

A few moments later, he stood in her doorway, staring at the framed motivational posters as if they might rearrange themselves into something that made sense.

"Come in, Fernando," Principal Nester said, not looking up from the folder on her desk.

He stepped inside. The office smelled like lemon cleaner and stale coffee. The blinds were half-closed, casting the room in pale afternoon light. He'd been in there a few times before, but it still made him nervous.

"You wanted to see me?"

Nester finally lifted her eyes. Her expression was careful, practiced. "Please, sit."

He sat.

She folded her hands over the folder. His name was printed across the tab in black marker. He recognized his own handwriting from the supply room—he'd labeled it himself at the beginning of the year, thinking it would sit in a cabinet collecting positive observations and commendations.

"I'll get straight to the point," she said. "The district has decided to terminate your employment immediately. Another teacher will take over your classes this year. You are to clear out your desk and leave after classes end today."

For a second, he genuinely thought he'd misheard her. "Leave? I've only been here two months."

"Yes."

"My early evaluation was exemplary."

"Yes." She inhaled slowly. "This decision isn't about performance."

He let out a short, disbelieving laugh. "Then what is it about?"

"There have been… concerns."

"From who?"

"The board."

He waited.

"Regarding your family history."

"My family history," he repeated. He closed his eyes and thought about the classroom he'd put so much effort into. The mismatched beanbags he'd bought with his own money. The shelf of dog-eared novels. The sign over the board that read Stories Matter.

"What concerns?" he pressed, anger building. He wanted to hear her say it.

Principal Nester hesitated, then chose her words carefully. "It's been brought to the district's attention that your past in New Mexico was quite sordid. We expect more from our teachers, as you well know. Your relation to Diego Medina is unacceptable. If parents were to find out, they would be outraged."

"I have nothing to do with his crimes."

"The board is under pressure, Fernando."

"Pressure," he echoed.

She looked tired now. Not cruel, but tired. "The parents of our students want the very best for their children. We cannot risk keeping someone related to a child molester. It is simply intolerable."

He took a breath, forcing himself to steady. "I have done nothing wrong."

Nester's eyes flicked down. "It's about optics," she said finally.

"Optics," he repeated again, as if tasting something rotten.

"The school board election is next month. There's been a lot of… attention." She lowered her voice. "If your past was discovered by the wrong people, you would become the focal point."

"You're firing me because some parents would be uncomfortable about something my uncle did. An uncle, by the way, that I am not in contact with," he said. "Do you think I would do something like him?"

"No one is saying that."

"You don't have to say it."

She flinched slightly.

"The official reason," she continued, retreating to formality, "is a restructuring of staff to better align with community values."

"Community values," he repeated, almost smiling at the absurd vagueness of it.

Her voice softened. "You will be an excellent teacher, Fernando."

"Then fight for me." The plea slipped out before he could stop it.

Her gaze held his, and for a moment, he saw the truth there. Fear. The fear of angry board members and loud parents. Of losing her own position.

"It's bigger than me," she said quietly. The clock on the wall ticked, loud and indifferent. "You'll receive severance through the end of the semester," she said. "We'll provide a neutral reference."

He straightened, the initial shock cooling into something steadier. "Fine, but I'm leaving now."

"I understand. For what it's worth, I'm sorry," she added, almost in a whisper.

"Oh, fuck your sorry." He gave her a hard look. "This isn't right, and you know it."

Then he opened the door and stepped into the hallway, where lockers slammed, and laughter sounded, and the world went on exactly the same as it had that morning.

He didn't know for sure who had called the board and told them about Fernando's uncle, but he could guess. It didn't matter anyway. He had done nothing wrong. He could fight the termination, but honestly, he didn't have the energy to do it.

He was completely numb as he quickly grabbed his belongings from his classroom and went to his car. A few other teachers tried to ask him what was happening, but he ignored them. He was so tired.

Back at home, he sat on the edge of his couch, the lamp in the corner casting a soft golden circle over the living room. The house felt too quiet without the television on, too aware of its own stillness.

"Come here, buddy," he murmured.

At the sound of his voice, Beans lifted his head from the rug. His tail thumped once, then twice, against the floor before he stood and padded over, nails clicking softly on the hardwood. He rested his chin on Fernando's knee first, looking up with those warm, patient eyes, as if asking to hear everything. Fernando smiled despite himself.

"You don't even know what kind of day I had," he said, scratching behind Beans's ear.

Beans huffed gently and leaned harder into his hand.

Fernando shifted back against the couch cushions and patted the space beside him. Beans climbed up in an awkward, enthusiastic tangle of paws and fur, circling once before settling half across Fernando's lap. He was far too big to be a lap dog, but neither of them seemed to mind.

He wrapped one arm around the dog, fingers sinking into thick, soft fur. Beans let out a deep, contented sigh that vibrated through his chest.

They stayed like that for a long moment, no words, just the steady rhythm of breathing. Fernando rested his cheek against the top of Beans's head, inhaling that familiar, clean-dog smell.

"You're the best part of this place," he said quietly. "Well, you and Walker."

Beans's tail thumped again, slower this time, as if in agreement.

Outside, a car passed, and somewhere outside, a door shut, but inside the living room, everything felt warm and safe. Fernando rubbed slow circles along Beans's side, feeling the rise and fall of each breath.

Beans stretched one paw across Fernando's chest and closed his eyes.

Fernando did too, and for the first time all day, the weight on his shoulders felt lighter, replaced by several pounds of loyal, steady comfort.

CHAPTER 17

A week later, Walker's unit finally got back to base. The barracks were quieter than usual for a Friday night. Most of the guys were down at the smoke pit or trying to sweet-talk someone on FaceTime.

Walker sat on the edge of his bed, staring at his phone. No calls or emails from Fernando for a full week. The faint echo of boots in the hallway came and went.

"Gunny talked to you yet?" Pug asked from his own spot sprawled across Walker's bed.

"Yeah," Walker said. "He brought up the bonus."

Pug huffed. "They're throwing numbers at me too, and acting like I'm crazy for even thinking about getting out."

Walker glanced at him. "You are thinking about it?"

Pug finally sat up. "Yeah. I am." He rubbed his hands together like he was trying to warm them. "Eight years, man. I missed my sister's wedding. My dad's surgery. I don't even know what my nephew's favorite color is."

Walker nodded slowly. "Blue. It's always blue."

Pug gave a weak laugh. "You know what I mean."

Outside, someone shouted, and a door slammed. The building settled again into a humming, fluorescent stillness.

"They keep talking about career," Pug went on. "About picking up staff, about twenty years, and a pension. I don't know."

Walker looked down at his phone again. "I joined at eighteen. Thought I'd do four and bounce. Then it turned into this."

"So what changed?"

Walker was quiet for a long moment. "Fernando and I went to visit his family. They're… I don't even know how to describe it. It was really nice."

Pug sat up and leaned forward, his elbows on his knees. "You thinking about moving there?"

"Yeah." Pug finally met his eyes. "We are." The words hung between them, and Walker couldn't help but feel disloyal. He had put off telling Pug for weeks now.

"You feel guilty?" Pug asked, eyes soft.

"Every day," Walker admitted. "I feel like I'm quitting on the guys, and I owe the Corps more than what I've given."

Pug nodded. "That's what gets me. You start to think leaving means you didn't love it enough."

Walker shook his head. "I love it. I just don't want it to be my whole life."

Pug breathed out slowly. "I got accepted to a university back home. Mechanical engineering. I didn't tell anyone here."

Walker blinked. "You serious?"

"Yeah."

Walker grinned. "You're going to be the only guy in class who knows how to field-strip a rifle."

Pug smirked. "That will be real useful in Calculus."

They both laughed.

"Whatever you do," Walker said, quietly holding out his hand, "you're still my brother."

Pug clasped it, grip firm and familiar. "Same."

They stood there for a second longer than usual. Outside, someone started up a truck in the parking lot. Life moved forward, with or without them.

"You scared?" Pug asked.

"Terrified."

Pug nodded. "Yeah. Me too." He let go of Walker's hand and stood up. "Let's go see your omega. I've missed Beans, and your apartment is better than here."

Walker grinned again and agreed. A moment later, he was on the road, Pug following his bike in his truck. Soon enough, the neighborhood rolled past, and he kept it easy, shifting smoothly, letting the road carry him home to Fernando.

Soon, they stood in front of the apartment door as Fernando unlocked it. The front door clicked shut with a soft thud, and Walker immediately heard it. Music swelled dramatically from the living room.

"Hmm." Walker dropped his keys into the bowl by the entryway. It wasn't just music. No, Walker knew this. This was belting. Full, unapologetic Broadway belting.

He shared a look with Pug, and they grinned when a dog howled in harmony as Fernando sang about unrequited love at the top of his lungs.

They rounded the corner slowly.

Fernando was on the couch. Curtains half-drawn. Only the blue flicker of the television lighting the room. Onscreen, *Les Misérables* was in full emotional devastation mode with Anne Hathaway's character mid-solo, eyes glassy with heartbreak.

Fernando's eyes were also glassy. He was holding Beans in his arms like a baby.

"…And I dreamed a dream…" the TV sang.

Fernando sniffed loudly, and Beans licked his cheek.

Walker cleared his throat. "Honey, I'm home. Pug is here to visit, too."

Fernando jumped like he'd been caught committing a felony. He fumbled for the remote but hit volume up instead. The orchestra swelled. "Damn it." He stabbed at buttons until the room fell silent.

Pug tsked and walked over to the couch. He pulled Beans out of Fernando's arms. "You shouldn't have to see this, sweet boy. Let's go for a walk."

Walker moved closer, noticing the half-empty box of tissues and the fuzzy blanket wrapped around his shoulders. A bowl of popcorn untouched.

Walker sat beside him, close enough that their knees touched. "What's going on?"

For a moment, Fernando didn't answer. His jaw tightened, the way it did when he was trying very hard not to feel something. "She loses everything, Walker, but she still hopes it'll get better." His voice cracked, and he winced. "The school fired me because of Uncle Diego."

"Fuck, sweetheart," Walker said gently. "I'm so sorry. Can we appeal it?"

"No, I don't want to bother with it." Fernando looked embarrassed. "I don't know why this stuff gets to me anymore."

"Because you're a human being with a pulse?"

He huffed out a weak laugh. "Welcome home. I'm sorry you had to see this."

"Don't be sorry. I'm glad I'm here." Walker reached for the remote and hit play. The song resumed softly. He shifted, tucking Fernando against his side and stealing part of the blanket. "I'm going to make Pug get us Chinese food. We can watch musicals all night."

Fernando sniffed. "If we're going to spiral into theatrical despair, we should watch *The Greatest Showman* next. We can cry and aggressively inspire ourselves." He gave Walker a sideways look. "You're not going to make fun of me if I sing along, are you?"

"Oh, I absolutely will," he said, kissing the top of Fernando's head. "So will Pug, but we'll do it lovingly."

Another sniffle escaped Fernando, but this time he didn't hide it. "By the way, I'm pregnant too."

Walker looked down at him slowly. Fernando wore a scowl, and his dark eyes almost seemed to dare Walker to say something negative.

"I took three tests," Fernando continued. "All of them said the same thing. I have a doctor's appointment next week to confirm, but I'm pregnant."

The word hung there. *Pregnant.*

Walker stared at his omega, then his mouth opened and closed. Confusion and panic filled him, but one thing kept him steady. Fernando was there too. "Are you okay?" he asked finally, voice quiet.

Fernando nodded quickly, then shook his head. "I don't know. I'm scared, and I didn't want to tell you over text or anything. I just... I wanted you here."

Walker let out a slow breath, running a hand through his hair. The silence stretched just long enough to be worrisome. Then he reached for Fernando and pulled him into a hug, one hand cradling the back of his head.

Fernando let out a shaky breath and pressed his face into Walker's shoulder.

"We're having a baby?" Walker whispered, the words sounding unreal.

Fernando nodded against him. "Yeah."

Walker leaned back just enough to look at him, his expression softening, something like awe creeping in.

"Wow." A small, almost disbelieving laugh escaped him. "That's big."

"Too big?" Fernando asked, searching his face.

He shook his head immediately. "No. Just big." He cupped Fernando's face in his hands. "We'll figure it out. Okay? Whatever this looks like, we'll figure it out together."

He quickly texted Pug to pick up food and a cake. They needed to celebrate.

CHAPTER 18

*W*alker grinned as he drove Fernando's tiny car into Hobson Hills. His omega looked at peace again, and Beans was happy with his head out the back window. As was Pug. The October air had a bite to it, sharp and clean.

"Tomorrow, I want to go to the bookstore with Valentina and Beans, then get a cinnamon roll at Zoe's place."

"Deal," Walker agreed easily. "Maybe with Janelle, too. I think she's one of my people."

Fernando smirked. "She is. You, her, and Pug will get into so much trouble."

"She's been thinking of another prank for Mal."

Fernando shook his head. "When will you all learn?"

"Never."

They only had a couple of days in Hobson Hills since they drove this time, but it had been worth it to bring Beans and Pug.

"Are you sure Grammy wanted us both out to the cranberry bog today?"

Walker nodded. "We're going there first thing. She wants

to show us something, and I want to see the berries now that they're ready to harvest. Maybe I'll even get to help her some."

Soon, they pulled into the small gravel space next to the bog. Grammy and Gramps were already there, standing together on the dock, snuggling.

The cranberry bog stretched out like a dark red lake beneath the sun. The forest nearby whispered secrets as the wind blew through the golden leaves, and he could see a small, old house close by in the trees.

"This is beautiful," Fernando said softly, eyes wide with awe. "I see why you like the bog."

They walked together to the docks, Beans excited to be out of the car. The large puppy ran to Gramps and Grammy, tail wagging, as he begged for pets.

"Oh, you're a good boy, aren't you?" Gramps asked, kneeling down to properly scratch Beans's sides.

Beans grinned and wiggled as if to say, *Of course, I am a good boy, Gerard. Now, get to scratching, sir.*

Grammy shook her head and tossed waders to all three of them. "Nice to see you, Pug. Now, let's get to work. These berries won't harvest themselves."

Gramps snuck her a look, then quickly scampered away with Beans. "I'll just take this pup for a walk. He's been in the car a long time."

"So have I," Pug said, giving their retreating figures a longing look."

Grammy gave them a stern look. "Now, we have work to do before I show you something special."

"Yes, ma'am," they all said, giving small salutes.

She laughed, then instructed them on how to harvest the berries. A light fog clung low over the bog, turning the whole field into a soft, silver dream. The wooden boards creaked under their boots as they hurried behind Grammy.

"Slow down, slow down," She laughed, adjusting her wool hat. "Cranberries won't run away."

"They look like they're floating," Pug said, leaning over the edge of the flooded bog.

The water was speckled with red as thousands of tiny crimson berries drifted on the surface like scattered jewels.

"That's the trick," Grammy said. "They float. That's how we gather them."

She stepped carefully into the shallow water, her tall rubber boots making gentle ripples. In her hands was a long wooden rake with curved teeth.

"First," she said, holding it up, "you loosen the berries from the vines." She dipped the rake into the water and gently combed through the plants beneath the surface. The water trembled, and more berries popped free, bobbing up to join the others.

"What the frick?" Fernando gasped in delight. "They're popping."

Grammy grinned. "That's the sound of October."

Walker crouched down and poked one berry. It drifted away slowly. "They're so red."

"Because they're finally ready," Grandma said, giving him a knowing look. She handed Fernando a rake. "Your turn."

Fernando waded beside her, tongue stuck out in concentration as he copied the motion. More berries floated up, and soon the water was crowded with berries.

Grammy pulled a floating boom, a long yellow barrier, across the bog, guiding the cranberries together into a thick red cluster. "Now we herd them," she explained. "Just like sheep."

Pug laughed. "Berry sheep."

With long nets, they slowly pushed the berries toward a pump at the edge of the bog. The machine hummed softly, sucking the floating fruit into a large crate.

Pug picked one up and held it carefully. "Can we eat them?"

Grandma chuckled. "Sure. Go ahead and give it a try."

He took a bite and immediately scrunched up his face. "That's so sour. Disgusting. How could you do this to me, woman?"

Walker and the others burst into laughter. "Serves you right," Walker said, shoving his friend.

"That's why we make sauce," Grammy said, chuckling. "And juice. And pies."

The fog began to lift as the sun climbed higher, lighting the bog so the cranberries glowed like rubies across the water.

Grammy leaned on her rake and looked out over the bog. "My Dad showed me this same thing," she said softly. "One October, years ago."

Walker looked up from where he worked. "Thank you for showing us this. It's so peaceful and straightforward. I love it."

Grammy smiled. "That makes me very happy, sweet boy."

Water lapped gently against the rubber waders as they moved slowly through the bog, their scoops pushing floating cranberries into long red ribbons.

Walker tried to keep up with Grammy, though her pace surprised him. For someone in her seventies, she moved through the water like she'd been doing it all her life. Which, he supposed, she had.

"Careful with the scoop," she said, glancing over to Fernando. "You go too fast, and you'll just push them away."

Walker adjusted his grip on the wooden handle and dipped the scoop into the water. He pulled it toward him slowly, watching the berries tumble into the wire basket.

"Good job, Walker. You're a pro at this." Grammy patted his shoulder.

"Really?" He smiled wistfully. "I could do this all day."

"That's longer than my grandkids ever lasted," she said with a chuckle. "They help because they have to, but they don't love it as you do."

"Maybe they won't mind if I help you now," he said. "We're moving here, you know."

Grammy hid a smile. "Gerard told me."

A gust of wind rippled across the bog, sending the floating cranberries shifting like tiny red marbles. They worked for a while in comfortable silence. The scrape of scoops and distant chatter from Fernando and Pug drifted across the water.

Finally, Walker said, "Did you enjoy doing this when you were a kid?"

"I did, through all the tough times and good," she replied. "Dad and I would tend it, then in the fall, family came out to help." She scooped another row of berries, guiding them into the boom. "They didn't complain, though," she added. "Back then, this meant Thanksgiving pies and keeping the farm running another year."

Walker nudged a cluster of berries toward her line. "Can I help each fall? After this year, I'll have a lot more free time."

"Well," she said, "someone's gotta keep the tradition alive."

Walker scooped another basketful of cranberries, watching them shine deep red against the gray water. "Maybe I will."

She smiled but didn't look at him, just kept working. "That would make me very happy."

After a while, about half the berries had been harvested. Grammy looked over them proudly. "You three did a very good job. Now, I think it's time I show you my surprise."

"Is it more work?" Pug asked, snickering. "Walker said you all stayed busy in Hobson Hills, and I'm starting to believe it."

"Eh." Grammy shrugged. "It kinda is more work."

They climbed back onto the dock and took off the waders, leaving them in a wet pile. Walker fully intended to come back and finish the harvest.

"This way," Grammy said, walking toward the house in the forest.

The building sat alone at the edge of the cranberry bog, looking like an exhausted grandparent. Its gray wooden siding had long ago lost whatever paint once protected it, leaving the boards silvered and rough from years of wind and rain. A narrow porch wrapped around the front, its railings crooked, one post braced by a weathered plank that looked almost as old as the house itself.

It was still picturesque, though. The cranberry vines stretched out in long red carpets across the low fields, their color deep and dark in the fading afternoon light, and behind the house, tall pines and maples stood close together, their leaves halfway through turning. Rust-colored maple leaves drifted lazily down, gathering along the porch steps and across the packed dirt path that led from the bog. The wind carried the smell of damp earth and cold water, the perfect autumn scent.

"The inside is a lot nicer," Grammy said, opening the door. "Come take a look."

Inside, smooth hardwood floors gleamed. A large living room, kitchen, and dining area lay open. The appliances looked brand new, shining silver. The counters were white with dark, swirling marble tops, and a small kitchen island sat in the middle of the space. A stack of papers lay there.

"There's a bathroom at the back," Grammy said, leading them through. "Come look upstairs."

One spacious room with a private bathroom was on one side, and two smaller rooms with a connecting bathroom were on the other.

One upstairs window of the house hung slightly open, its screen rattling faintly whenever the wind picked up. The glass panes were uneven and old, warping the view of the bog beyond them so the red fields seemed to ripple even when the air was still.

The place had the quiet of age. Somewhere that had seen many seasons come and go. Beyond it all, the cranberry bog stretched toward the hayfield, while the old house kept its silent watch at the edge of the field.

"Wow," Fernando said, looking around. The inside is gorgeous, Grammy. You all did a really nice job fixing it up."

"We were motivated with love." Grammy smiled softly. "Mateo, Abel, and Valentina helped a lot, too."

Fernando snorted. "I can see why Mateo and Abel would help, but Valentina doesn't do manual labor if she can help it."

"She wanted you and Walker to have a nice home."

Walker and Fernando both froze in place, staring at Grammy.

Pug started laughing. "I knew it! This is great. The baby can have this room, and I'll take the other when I come to visit. Beans will really like it here. He can do his business all over the place."

"You'll sell us this house?" Walker asked, surprised. He had money saved up so they could do a down payment easily. "How much are you thinking?"

"Zero." Grammy shrugged. "It's been here longer than Gerard, and I have. No one in the family was interested in it, but I wanted to keep it just in case. And here we are. I have a new grandson who needs a home and who happens to like working in the cranberry bog."

"Grammy," he said, shocked.

Fernando was already wiping his eyes. "Really? I'll help in the bog too when you need me, Grammy."

She shook her head. "Nope. I'll be helping you two. The bog comes with the house. You can provide berries to Farm Fresh and sell them at the farmer's market every weekend in the fall. I usually make a tidy little sum. It will be a nice supplement for you two."

"Grammy," Walker said again, tears filling his eyes.

"You're family now, Walker." She hugged him close, and he got that mysterious warm feeling again. He knew what it was now. It was love.

THE NEXT DAY, Fernando left Grammy and Walker in the cranberry bog. The two got along a little too well, if he was being honest. Walker might pick up some bad habits.

Fernando fought a grin.

The middle school auditorium smelled faintly of dust, old curtains, and fresh paint. Ms. Bautista stood at the edge of the stage holding a clipboard while a dozen theater students sat scattered across the first few rows. Some leaned across the seats talking, a few were already flipping through scripts, and one kid in the back was trying to balance a pencil on his upper lip.

"Alright, alright, settle down," Ms. Bautista called, clapping twice. Her voice echoed through the empty theater.

The chatter slowly faded.

"I have someone I want you all to meet." She turned toward where he stood in the wings and gestured.

Fernando stepped out from behind the curtain, feeling slightly overwhelmed by the size of the room. He wore jeans and a faded band T-shirt, and carried a stack of folders awkwardly pressed to his chest.

"This," Ms. Bautista said, smiling, "is Mr. Medina. He'll be teaching English next year, but for now, he's going to be substitute teaching and helping out with the theater club."

Fernando lifted a hand in a small wave. "Hi."

One of the seniors in the front row squinted at him. "Helping how?"

"Everything," Ms. Bautista said immediately. "Sets, rehearsals, tech week, costume runs, the occasional emotional breakdown."

A few students laughed.

Fernando chuckled nervously. "Hopefully not my emotional breakdown."

"No promises," someone muttered from the back. Fernando recognized the boy Valentina had a crush on.

Oh, we'll be spending a lot of time together, he thought, maniacal laughter filling his mind.

Ms. Bautista continued. "Mr. Medina just graduated from university, where he minored in theater. He was brave enough to volunteer his afternoons with you, chaos goblins."

"Hey!" a girl called out.

"Accurate though," Valentina's crush agreed, shrugging.

Fernando stepped forward a little, still clutching the folders. "I did a lot of stage management and lighting in college. I also built sets, painted backdrops, and once had to fix a prop door five minutes before opening night."

"Did it work?" Valentina's crush asked.

"Barely."

That got a few more laughs.

Ms. Bautista nodded toward the stage. "He's going to help us with this year's winter and spring shows, which means you'll be seeing him a lot."

The boy with the pencil raised his hand without removing it from his lip.

Ms. Bautista sighed. "Yes, Trevor."

The pencil dropped. "Does he sing?"

Fernando blinked. "Uh… not well. I usually stay back-house." Gigi and Nolan were the ones who liked acting, singing, and dancing. Well, he liked it, but wasn't exactly great at it.

Trevor leaned back in his seat. "Good. Less competition."

A girl with a script grinned. "We'll make him sing by February."

Fernando looked at Ms. Bautista. "Is that… a thing that happens?"

"Oh, absolutely," she said cheerfully.

The students started murmuring again, but this time with curious energy.

Ms. Bautista clapped once more.

"Alright. Welcome Mr. Medina properly by not scaring him off on day one."

Trevor raised his hand again.

"No more questions," she said.

Trevor lowered it slowly.

"I WAS gonna ask if he believed in ghosts," the boy muttered.

Ms. Bautista groaned.

Fernando glanced up toward the dark catwalks above the stage. "Should I?" he asked.

Half the theater kids immediately started talking at once.

CHAPTER 19

*S*ix months later

THE LIVING ROOM smelled faintly like lavender and microwave popcorn. Fernando sat in the middle of the couch with a blanket tucked around his legs, feeling both amused and slightly overwhelmed. His eight-month-pregnant belly stretched the soft fabric of his T-shirt, and a mountain of pillows had somehow appeared around him. Iggy sat cuddled on one side of him, and Emma sat on the other. *Wicked* played on television.

"I feel like royalty," he said.

"You are royalty," Mateo replied from the kitchen. He carried a tray with a bowl of cut fruit, crackers, and a suspiciously large slice of chocolate cake. "The King of Babyland."

Fernando laughed. "That's not a real place. Damn, you're so cheesy. I think I'm infected with it now, too."

"Babyland is real today," Mateo said, setting the tray in

front of him like a waiter in a fancy restaurant. "Your Majesty's lunch."

In front of the couch, Valentina sat cross-legged on the floor with a bottle of black nail polish. "Don't move your feet," she warned. "I don't want to accidentally paint your foot."

Fernando tried to look over his belly. "You guys don't have to do all this. Walker will be here for good tomorrow. I can handle myself for one day."

Walker would be leaving the base for the last time tomorrow morning. They had already given up their apartment lease and moved everything up to Hobson Hills. It had been hard going back and forth the past six months, but soon, that wouldn't be a problem anymore.

"Too late," Valentina said. "We've already committed."

Beans lay beside her and began to pre-clean one of Fernando's feet.

"Beans, you are disgusting." Fernando sighed.

The front door opened, and Gabriela stepped in carrying three grocery bags. "I bring offerings," she announced.

"Wahasht?" Fernando asked as he took a large bite of cake.

Mateo peeked inside one bag. "Ice cream?"

"Three kinds," Gabriela said proudly. "Chocolate, strawberry, and that weird pickle one you said pregnant people like."

Fernando stared at her. "That was a joke, Gabs."

She paused. "So nobody wants pickle ice cream?"

Valentina burst out laughing. "Seriously? They make that?"

Mateo clapped her on the shoulder. "Hermanita, you got played."

Fernando leaned back into the pillows, smiling at the chaos around him.

Valentina gently lifted his foot and began painting his toenails with exaggerated care. "You know," she said, "once the baby gets here, we expect visitation rights."

"Visitation rights?" Fernando said.

"Absolutely," Gabriela said, digging spoons out of a drawer. "We're the cool aunts."

Mateo pointed at himself. "What about me? I'm a cool uncle."

Gabriela sniffed. "Sure, you are."

"I'm teaching the kid how to ride a bike."

"Before they can walk?" Gabriela asked.

"Early training," Mateo said.

Fernando shook his head, laughing softly. For a moment, he rested his hands on his belly.

The baby kicked.

"Oh!" he said.

All three siblings froze.

"What?" Valentina said immediately.

"Did it move?" Gabriela asked, already kneeling beside the couch.

Fernando nodded, smiling wider now. "Yeah. Right here."

Mateo crouched and placed a careful hand on his stomach.

Emma pressed her ear to his side, and Iggy's small hand settled beside Mateo's.

The room went quiet.

A second later, the baby kicked again.

Iggy's eyes widened. "Whoa."

"That's so weird," Valentina whispered, grinning.

Fernando looked at all three of them crowding around him, their faces full of amazement. "You guys are going to spoil this kid," he said.

Mateo shrugged. "Runs in the family."

Later that night, Fernando finally got rid of his siblings

and had some peace and quiet. He loved the old creaks and moans of their new home. They had used some of Walker's savings to put new siding on the house and replace the windows and doors. The porch had been rebuilt, bigger and better. The cranberry bog was dry now, vines green and new.

The front door creaked open before a knock even finished echoing through the house.

Fernando froze in the kitchen, a dish towel still clutched in his hands. For a moment, he thought he imagined it—the sound, the shift of air, the quiet footsteps on the hardwood floor.

"Hello?" a familiar voice called.

The towel slipped from his fingers.

Fernando stepped closer to the front door, heart pounding so loudly he could hear it in his ears.

Standing just inside the doorway, duffel bag slung over one shoulder, was Walker. He looked thinner. Tired. His hair was shorter than he remembered. That smile, though. Soft, unsure, and hopeful. It was exactly the same.

For a second, neither of them moved.

"Hey," Walker said quietly, eyes on Fernando's belly.

Fernando's breath hitched. "You said tomorrow."

"I know," he said with a small shrug. "Thought I'd surprise you."

That was all it took. He crossed the room in a heartbeat, throwing his arms around Walker so hard it nearly knocked the duffel bag off his shoulder.

Walker let out a startled laugh before wrapping his arms around Fernando, holding him just as tightly.

Fernando buried his face in Walker's chest, breathing in the familiar smell of laundry soap and dust and something that was just him. "You're here," he whispered, his voice breaking. "You're actually here."

"I'm here," Walker murmured, pressing his cheek to the top of his head.

During another long deployment, this time for humanitarian purposes, their conversations had been through screens and phone calls. Grainy video chats where the signal froze at the worst moments. Short texts that tried to hold entire feelings inside a few words.

Now there was no delay. Just warmth. Solid and real.

Fernando pulled back slightly, his hands cupping Walker's face as if he needed proof that he wasn't about to disappear again. "You're okay?"

Walker nodded. "Yeah."

"You're really okay?"

Walker smiled softly. "I am now."

Fernando laughed through tears and hugged him again.

From the living room, Beans suddenly exploded into barking, skidding across the hardwood floor before launching himself at Walker's legs.

"Well, hey there, buddy." Walker laughed, dropping the duffel bag to crouch down as the dog licked his face enthusiastically.

Fernando leaned against the wall, watching the two of them with watery eyes and a smile he couldn't stop. He didn't mention that Beans had been licking his feet earlier.

Walker looked up at him. "Missed you," he said.

Fernando walked over and took his hand, squeezing it tight. "Good," he replied softly. "Because you're not leaving again for a very long time."

He stood, pulling Fernando into his arms once more, holding him like he meant it. "I'm never leaving again."

EPILOGUE

A few weeks later, Walker's new truck rolled slowly up the gravel driveway, its tires crunching softly as the engine idled down. The sun was beginning to sink behind the tree line, spilling warm orange light across the cranberry bog. Dust clung to the sides of the truck, the same way it clung to Walker.

He turned the engine off and sat there for a moment, hands resting on the steering wheel. His shoulders ached in that deep, satisfying way that only came from a long day of physical labor. He flexed his fingers, feeling the stiffness from hours of gripping tools, hauling feed, and fixing fence posts that refused to cooperate.

Today, Walker, handyman extraordinaire, worked with Marco Wilson on his ranch. After a long day, the man's cattle had settled, the chickens were already hopping onto their roosts, and the steady hum of cicadas filled the evening air. *A good day*, he thought, smiling. Tomorrow, he would be working at Abel's brewery. His machinery needed a little tender loving care. With his new career, each day was different with a new challenge, and he loved it.

He pushed open the truck door and stepped out, boots hitting the dirt with a dull thud. His jeans were streaked with soil, his shirt damp with sweat and dust. He stretched his back, wincing slightly before letting out a long breath.

From the porch, the screen door creaked open. "There you are."

Walker looked up to see Fernando leaning against the doorway, arms crossed but smiling softly. He was due to give birth any moment now. Their family would soon have a little girl named Juanita Medina.

Beans wiggled out past Fernando and barked happily, dancing around Walker. Their son was almost fully grown now – a big, fuzzy boy with no manners or sense of boundaries. *Best boy ever*, Walker thought as he bent to hug the large dog.

Looking up, Walker noticed the porch light glowing behind Fernando, and the smell drifting from the house. His stomach growled. "Smells like dinner from Gil's place," he said, walking toward the steps.

"Pot roast," Fernando replied, wiggling his brows. "I figured you'd be starving after working with Marco all day."

Walker climbed the steps slowly, every muscle reminding him exactly how long the day had been.

When he reached the porch, Fernando gave him a quick once-over. "You look like the cows won."

Walker chuckled, wiping his hands on his jeans. "They tried. The buggers wouldn't leave me alone while I worked on the fence. I had to hand out treats to get any peace."

Fernando reached up and brushed a streak of dirt from Walker's cheek with his thumb. "You clean up, and I'll put our dinner on plates. We can pretend it's home-cooked."

Walker leaned against the doorframe for a second, looking out across the darkening woods. The wind rolled softly through the trees. It had been a long day, but he was finally home.

AFTERWORD

If you would like to keep up with releases, please like and follow me on Instagram (@c.w._gray) or Facebook (@cwgrayauthor), join C.W. Gray's Reading Nook on Facebook, or visit my website at https://cwgray-author.com. You can also have early access to my work on Patreon:

(https://www.patreon.com/c/cwgrayauthor)

www.ingramcontent.com/pod-product-compliance
Lightning Source LLC
Chambersburg PA
CBHW050006040726
47599CB00014B/1241